## A MAN MAY OFFER

He was taken aback when Miss Rosie smiled and said, "I am endlessly amazed how men seem to dread the wedding ceremony when they are the ones who propose marriage in the first place."

"In the *first* place," he said, leaning his elbows on the table as he caught her eyes, determined not to let them escape him again, "a man may offer a proposal of marriage. However, I have spoken with many gentlemen who assure me that they found themselves making that offer simply because it seemed the proper thing to do when the lady had turned the discussion in that direction."

"So you wish us to believe that men propose marriage only because they are cornered into it?" She laughed.

Jo Ann Ferguson has written more than 50 romances for Zebra, including . . .

*A Kiss for Mama*
*A Kiss for Papa*
*A Valentine Waltz*
*His Unexpected Bride*
*Murder at Almack's*
*Valentine Kittens*
*Wedding Day Kittens*

The Dunsworthy Brides:
*The Perfect Bride*
*A Primrose Wedding*

Priscilla Flanders mysteries:
*A Rather Necessary End*
*Grave Intentions*
*Faire Game*
*The Greatest Possible Mischief*
*Digging Up Trouble*
*The Wedding Caper*

# A PRIMROSE WEDDING

## Jo Ann Ferguson

ZEBRA BOOKS
Kensington Publishing Corp.
www.kensingtonbooks.com

ZEBRA BOOKS are published by

Kensington Publishing Corp.
850 Third Avenue
New York, NY 10022

All Kensington titles, imprints, and distributed lines are available at special quantity discounts for bulk purchases for sales promotion, premiums, fund-raising, educational, or institutional use.

Special book excerpts or customized printings can also be created to fit specific needs. For details, write or phone the office of the Kensington Special Sales Manager: Attn. Special Sales Department. Kensington Publishing Corp., 850 Third Avenue, New York, NY 10022. Phone: 1-800-221-2647.

Zebra and the Z logo Reg. U.S. Pat. & TM Off.

ISBN 0-8217-7842-0

First Printing: August 2005
10 9 8 7 6 5 4 3 2 1

Printed in the United States of America

*For Donna*
*Who always danced to her own music—*
*And invited everyone to join in.*

# PROLOGUE

It was a simple church in an ordinary English village. Only one thing made it unique. Saints promenading in an orderly row had been carved into one wall of the church at a spot that was hidden from the green and the road that cut through the village. The saints' faces had been bearded with moss and edged with thorns of climbing roses. At their feet were the words that had been etched into the stone centuries before:

*Once, twice, thrice—*
*Be it by heaven or by the devil's own device*
*What joy or grief for one shall be worthy*
*Shall come the same for each Dunsworthy*

# CHAPTER ONE

The rain had faded to a mist when Rosie Dunsworthy stepped out of the butcher's shop in the small village of Dunstanbury. A quartet of other shops edged the narrow road that sliced through the village and led to the hills beyond. Across the green, the church's ancient tower interrupted the arc of a rainbow that vanished beyond the curtain wall of Dunsworthy Hall.

"You even have the pot of gold now, don't you, cousin?" Rosie asked.

She chided herself, glad that no one had been privy to her childish question. Truly, she was happy that she no longer had to live in that creaking, musty hall. She would have gladly remained there, however, if it meant her brother had not been killed in the war with Napoleon.

But the war was over, and the early autumnal day had just the right amount of chill to need a cloak but not a coat. This was her favorite season of the year. With all the colors about to burst forth on the trees growing on the hills around Dunstanbury, she could imagine she was in the midst of a glorious painting.

Checking that the bright red linen was tucked

over her purchases from the butcher, she shifted her other basket, where a special treat for her aunt waited beneath a checkered cloth. Aunt Millicent adored Mrs. Hanover's red raspberry preserves, so Rosie had brought some fresh eggs from Dunsworthy Dower Cottage to trade for a jar. The smell of bread baking had filtered through the cottage when Rosie was putting on her cloak to come into Dunstanbury. Tonight they would feast on fresh bread and red raspberry preserves.

A song bubbled up through her, a happy tune that seemed to banish the dampness and swirl through her with the anticipation of the good supper they would enjoy tonight. She let the melody slip past her lips, but softly, so nobody else would hear each note. Her steps lightened as the song coming from her imagination teased her to whirl about.

She laughed as quietly as she had been humming. If she danced across the green, she would be labeled mad. She could almost hear the whispers.

*Did you hear that the younger Miss Dunsworthy was capering about the green? Do you think she is quite right? She seldom says much, and now she is dancing when there is no music.*

Rosie drew the hood of her dark red cloak up over her straw bonnet and bowed her head to avoid the water dripping from the trees edging the green. Her left slipper flooded when she stepped into a puddle thick with leaves.

Grimacing, she shook her foot. She should concentrate on where she was going rather than letting her mind drift to tonight's supper. The song burst into her head again. Music was always her companion, but never more so than since her sister had married. Rosie had not guessed how much she would miss Bianca.

With a laugh to get rid of her grim thoughts, she swung the baskets in rhythm with her steps as she crossed the damp green. She would not take a short cut through the fields as she often did, because the ground was soaked from the rain. Even the rutted and muddy road would be better.

Few voices drifted through the late afternoon. Lamps shone through windows of the village's thatch-roofed cottages. As she walked past, she waved to people in open doorways. No one wanted to be trapped in their house until winter arrived. Then, the cold winds off the sea that edged the road leading toward Dunsworthy Dower Cottage would be merciless, and every hearth in the shire would be crowded.

Rosie heard the carriage before it came into view. She climbed onto the church steps to keep from being splashed. If it was the Mail, it was hours late. It should have passed through Dunstanbury before midday. Maybe something was amiss because, from the sounds, its speed was slower than usual.

The carriage came into view. In disbelief, she stared at it. Not the Mail, but she recognized it with ease, because she had ridden in it less than a pair of fortnights ago. What was Lucian's carriage doing in Dunstanbury now? The earl and his new bride had not returned from their honeymoon on the Continent, and she could not imagine why their carriage would be in Dunstanbury this afternoon.

The coachman waved to her, and Rosie, setting one basket on the steps, waved back. Moss loved driving the carriage. She would always remember how thoughtful he had been to her. His dark hair and simple green livery were damp from the rain, but his eyes were as bright as morning sunshine.

"Good afternoon, Miss Dunsworthy!" he called.

"Welcome back to Dunstanbury. I—" Rosie had thought nothing could amaze her more than seeing Moss and the carriage today, but, as a man on horseback came from behind the carriage, she realized she was wrong. Before she could halt herself, she blurted, "Lord Fortenbury, what are you doing in Dunstanbury?"

She put her fingers to her lips, halting herself from asking another want-witted question. Thank heavens, Aunt Millicent was not privy to this conversation! Her aunt would lament Rosie's lack of sense in speaking so to the viscount.

Lord Fortenbury threaded his chestnut horse between the carriage and the steps. His height in the saddle made him an impressive sight, especially when his navy riding coat was lathered by rain to his arms, accenting every muscle. Beneath his hat, like the rest of his clothing in prime twig, his dark hair was twisting into tight curls.

He swung down off the horse and drew off his riding gloves, which were only a shade lighter than his hair. "Good afternoon, Miss Primrose."

Rosie fought not to frown when Lord Fortenbury used her given name. She hated it. Such a silly name for a grown woman! Her mother had been sensible, everyone said. Why had she given her younger daughter such an absurd name? Mayhap her father had chosen it. If so, he had been as mistaken in that choice as he had been with the many foolish wagers that had left the family destitute.

When the viscount bowed over her hand, she stiffened. Everyone in Dunstanbury must be watching and measuring how her work-gown was no complement for Lord Fortenbury's clothes, which suggested he had just come from his tailor. When he drew her hand up to his mouth, he lowered it without kissing it, looking past her.

She turned and motioned for Constable Powers to join them by the church's steps. The blond constable's brawny strength warned any scofflaw in Dunstanbury to think twice before breaking the law. Davis, as he preferred for her to call him in hopes that she would consider his suit, had won a weight-lifting contest at a market day in the next town, lifting almost twice as much as any of his competitors. Never had he been anything but kind to her. Mayhap if she were less shy and he bolder, they would have exchanged more than a handful of words each time they met.

His customary smile was missing, replaced by lowered brows and a frown. "Do you know these men, Miss Rosie?" he asked.

"Yes, Constable Powers."

He waited for her to continue, but the words, as happened too often, seemed stuck to the roof of her mouth.

Lord Fortenbury said, "I am Rupert Jordan."

Davis nodded, although Rosie could tell by his puzzled expression that the name meant nothing to him. He looked up at Moss. "Aren't you Lord Wandersee's coachman?"

"Yes, sir. My name is Moss."

"You have been in Dunstanbury before."

Moss nodded.

"Then you should know that the good folks of Dunstanbury appreciate carriages slowing down when they enter the village." The constable continued to frown.

Rosie did not want to agree, for that would put Moss in a difficult situation. He had been driving far slower than the Mail did when passing through Dunstanbury, but this carriage was swifter than her neighbors' carts.

Before she could think of something to say that would not be a lie, because she could not imagine speaking falsely when she stood on the church steps, Lord Fortenbury stepped forward.

The viscount's smile did not waver as he said, "I trust, from your words, that you are the constable."

"Constable Powers." He clasped his hands behind his dusty brown coat and tapped the toe of one worn boot against the steps.

"You are right, Constable Powers."

"I am?" choked Constable Powers.

Sympathy surged up through Rosie. For a moment, albeit a brief moment, Constable Powers had been more assertive than she had ever seen him. Lord Fortenbury's agreement seemed to deflate him.

"Both Moss and I will endeavor," the viscount answered, "not to speed through Dunstanbury again. We have traveled from Bath, and I have to own that we were eager to reach our journey's end. Thank you for your understanding."

"Make sure there is no further need for me to be understanding." The constable's mouth tightened.

Rosie recognized that expression. She wondered why Constable Powers was acting as if he wanted to start a brangle with Lord Fortenbury.

"I will make quite sure of that," Lord Fortenbury said.

When the constable walked away across the green,

she was tempted to apologize to the viscount. What could she possibly say? No one had done anything wrong. Constable Powers had been right to caution Moss and the viscount. Lord Fortenbury had been gracious. Why had the situation become uncomfortable?

"A good man," Lord Fortenbury continued as he watched Constable Powers walk away.

"Yes." *That* she could agree with.

"I have explained my arrival in Dunstanbury to his satisfaction. Now I collect I should do the same for you." He picked up the basket she had placed on the steps and slipped it over his arm as he offered his other hand to assist her down the stairs. Looking about, he said, "This is a pleasing village."

Following his gaze, she admired Dunstanbury. The buildings were simple but had an aura of time past. With their fronts in good repair, the shops were welcoming. Even when her brother had been alive and the family had resided at Dunsworthy Hall, she had looked forward to any opportunity to come into the village to visit the shops and see the children who lived in the nearby cottages.

"I have always enjoyed it," she replied when she saw he was waiting for an answer. Getting those words out had not been as difficult as she had expected.

"It is quiet."

"That it is." She laughed, amazed that she could. "Some would say it is too quiet."

"Would you say that?"

How easy he was to talk to! She had found him so when she first met him in Plymouth almost a month ago but in the intervening days had begun to question if she had imagined how facile their few brief conversations had been.

"No, but I am accustomed to Dunstanbury. I have lived here all my life."

He smiled, and she wondered what she had said that pleased him. She did not know much about him . . . other than what Lucian had told her. She knew that Lord Fortenbury had a deep interest in relics from Egypt, for they had discussed that during the weekend hosted by his brother. Otherwise, she had discovered only that he was an excellent dancer and a genial host along with his brother, who was getting married within the fortnight.

"You are fortunate, Miss Primrose."

"Rosie, if you would please, my lord."

"But Primrose is a lovely name for a lady who is as pretty as the blossom."

She hoped she was not blushing. When she heard a smothered sound, she noticed Moss trying not to laugh.

Lord Fortenbury must have heard as well, because he asked, "Do you find my compliments to Miss Primrose amusing, Moss?" He glanced at her and winked. "Miss Rosie, I mean."

She hid her shock at his untoward motion. Looking at the coachman, who was losing his battle to restrain his laughter, she said, "Mayhap it is as simple as Moss has seen the jar of preserves in the basket you are holding, my lord, and is eager to sample a bite."

Pulling back the cloth, the viscount asked, "Is this of your making?"

"No."

"Will you tell me who made it?" he asked when she added nothing else.

Rosie hated her own shyness, but she never had found a way to overcome it. Forcing out the words made her stutter, and she hated that even more. Somehow she managed to say, "M-M-Mrs. H-H-Hanover."

"I have heard you are skilled in the kitchen. Therefore, I must assume Mrs. Hanover makes the best jams and preserves in Dunstanbury."

She nodded.

"May I try a bit for myself?"

In her head, she heard Aunt Millicent scolding her for failing to welcome the viscount as she should. She still did not look at him as she said, "Aunt Millicent and I would be delighted to have you join us for supper." Raising her eyes, she glanced toward the carriage. "Moss, you are, of course, welcome at Dunsworthy Dower Cottage as well."

"We accept." Lord Fortenbury opened the carriage door with a flourish and set the basket on the floor. He took the other one from her and put it inside as well. Holding out his hand, he said, "We are well met. I had not looked forward to the idea of presenting myself as a petitioner at your aunt's door."

"You were bound for Dunsworthy Dower Cottage?" Rosie asked, shocked out of her discomfort.

"Yes." Lord Fortenbury scanned the village green again. Several villagers had emerged from their homes to gape at the carriage that had visited Dunstanbury for the first time barely a month ago.

"What are they pointing at?" he asked.

"The carriage—"

"No, they are pointing to the far side of the church."

Rosie groaned inwardly. How could she explain that silly poem to him? Bianca had teased her about it on the day she wed Lucian, but Rosie found the whole legend embarrassing. Just because Bianca had fallen in love and married a fine lord did not mean that Rosie would have the same destiny. Bianca enjoyed such sallies as the carved poem, but Rosie hated it because it called unwanted attention to the rest of the Dunsworthy family.

When she did not answer, the viscount said, "Mayhap I should look for myself."

"No!" She grabbed his arm. She released it just as quickly when he smiled at her. Fire scorched her face, and she knew she was blushing. How she hated her red hair and the complexion that revealed every time she was overmastered! Which was far too often.

"Is it something I should not see?"

"It is nothing. Just an old engraving that folks around here are superstitious about."

"An old engraving?" His eyes lit with interest. "How old?"

"Not very old compared with the hieroglyphics you study, my lord." She cursed herself for using the word *old*. She should have guessed it would pique his interest, because he was as fascinated with the picture carvings from Egypt as she was.

He chuckled. "Now fingers are pointing toward the carriage as well. Does this old carving have something to do with Lucian's carriage?"

"To own the truth, yes."

"What?" His eyes grew wide.

"It can foretell just about every event that occurs in Dunstanbury."

"Ah, now I understand," he replied, although his expression suggested just the opposite. He took a step toward the side of the church where the engraving was almost hidden by grass. When rain began falling, heavier than before, he gave a regretful sigh. She doubted she was supposed to hear it because he was smiling as he held out his hand again and asked, "May I hand you into the carriage?"

"Thank you." She looked at Moss, who was giving her a bolstering smile. Had the coachman seen the engraving when he was last in Dunstanbury? Had Lucian or Bianca said something to him about it? She knew Lucian was well aware of that ludicrous poem, because he had not been surprised when Bianca was teasing her about it at their wedding. Quite the contrary, he had been smiling broadly as he squeezed Bianca's waist, suggesting a secret between him and his new wife.

Not that it mattered, as long as Lord Fortenbury was prevented from seeing it. She did not want for him to think that she, in any way, believed that ridiculous suggestion that what happened to one Dunsworthy happened to all of them. How could she when her older brother, Kevin, had died during the Peninsular War, and she and Bianca and Aunt Millicent still lived?

"Thank you," she murmured again when the viscount assisted her into the familiar carriage. Setting her baskets on the backward-facing seat, she reached to close the door.

He put out his hand to block the door. "May I join you in the carriage, Miss Rosie? I have had enough of today's cold, damp ride."

Rosie nodded, sure she would fumble over the words when excitement trilled through her. She truly enjoyed speaking with Lord Fortenbury. She had to remember that, and mayhap the words would not be reluctant to leave her lips.

She watched through the window as the viscount led his horse to the back of the carriage. When he vanished from sight, she assumed he was lashing the reins to the carriage. He returned quickly, and she slid away from the window, not wanting him to catch her peeking at him like a child.

"Bother. This seems determined to escape from my pocket." Lord Fortenbury bent toward the ground and then held up a ball whose outer layer was clearly made of fish skin.

"What is it?" she asked as he stepped into the carriage and sat where she had been sitting only a moment before. He closed the door behind him, then slapped the side of the carriage.

"My pocket globe."

"I am afraid that still does not answer my question, my lord."

Opening the ball, he handed it to her. "Take care, please."

"I will." She withdrew another ball from within the case and turned it slowly. "Why, it *is* a miniature of the whole earth."

"As far as explorers have traveled." He tilted the case. "Do you know what these dots represent?"

"The night sky. I recognize the constellations."

He took the pocket globe back from her. "I like to use it to judge how far I have traveled."

"Across England?"

"Anywhere I have or will travel. I find my curiosity leading me in many directions. Don't you?" Before she could given him an answer, even if she had had one, he faced her and said, "I trust that you do not think me too presumptuous to share your carriage."

"Of course not," she answered quickly.

"I have been in the saddle for two days, and I am pleased to allow Moss to do the driving." He leaned back against the seat, shifting his broad shoulders as if trying to make them comfortable. "Usually I enjoy riding Osiris—"

"You named your horse for the Egyptian god of the dead?"

"Osiris also ruled the earth." He smiled. "It seemed an appropriate name for a beast that travels upon it."

She could not disagree with that nor could she say that she was fascinated how he had let his studies slip into other aspects of his life.

"Listen to me," he said with a laugh. "How astonished Henry would be to hear me chattering like a gabble grinder!" He put the pocket globe beneath his coat. "My brother despairs of my ever speaking out on any topic in the House of Lords."

"Mayhap because nothing there transfixes you as the attempt to translate hieroglyphics does."

"You are most insightful, Miss Rosie. I shall have to remember that if I am attempting to keep anything from you."

"And what would that be?" Again she felt the all-too-familiar heat climbing up her cheeks. "Forgive me, my lord. I should not have asked such a personal question."

"You did not overstep the boundaries of propriety. I doubt you ever do."

Rosie smiled. "Now I must accuse you of being insightful, my lord."

"You are right. For example, I know right now that you are pleased not to have to walk home through the puddles."

"My exuberance at that may account for why I am talkative."

"Or it may be that you are pleased to see me."

Rosie lowered her eyes. He was *too* perceptive.

Knowing that, she must answer honestly. "That is true, my lord. I have enjoyed reading the books on Egypt that you lent me when we last spoke, and I have anticipated the opportunity to discuss them with you."

"You have read all three of those massive volumes since the assembly at my brother's house?"

"Yes, and I have learned much."

"Then I look forward to speaking with you about Egyptian artifacts."

As the carriage turned onto the road that followed the shore, wind tugged at Rosie's bonnet. She grasped the brim before the wind could peel it off her head. An arm stretched past her, and she leaned back as Lord Fortenbury lowered the shades on the sea side of the carriage.

"There is no need to do that," she said, "if you would like to view the sea as we pass."

"No need? You are fighting to keep your bonnet from flying away."

"My fault. I did not tie the ribbons tightly enough." Redoing the bow beneath her chin, she raised the curtains again. "I may have lived here all my life, but I never tire of watching the sea, except when it storms. Then I prefer to be safe and warm within Dunsworthy Dower Cottage."

"As you wish."

Rosie hesitated, knowing that she might seem overly bold. But she could not deny her curiosity any longer. She asked the question he had not answered before, "Lord Fortenbury, what *are* you doing here?"

# CHAPTER TWO

Rupert Jordan, fifth Lord Fortenbury, would have owned to no one, even himself, how relieved he was that the carriage's slowing kept him from having to reply to Miss Primrose Dunsworthy's question. Had she sensed that he was not here simply to give her and her aunt a look-in? She *was* insightful, and he had become quickly aware of her intelligence when she had called at his brother's house in Plymouth last month. Her keen mind was why he had lent her several of his most treasured books, the very books that he refused to allow anyone else to touch.

He had first been introduced to the pretty redhead by his good friend Lucian Wandersee when the Dunsworthy sisters and their aunt had arrived at Jordan Court, the home of his brother, Henry, for a gathering to begin the celebration of his brother's nuptials. Actually Henry had not been getting married for a few more weeks, but he had decided to have the longest running wedding party in history. Their friends had been eager to accept such an absurd—in Rupert's opinion—invitation because, with the Season past, any excuse for a gathering was welcome.

Rupert had been reluctant to become involved in the whole ludicrous assembly, preferring to continue his studies at Fortenbury Park, the family's acres near Bath. He had gone to Plymouth and his brother's house only because of Henry's insistence that Rupert, as current holder of the family's title, must be in attendance or Henry's betrothed's family would be insulted. Rupert had packed some of his favorite books and a few of the hieroglyphic tablets he had purchased. He had hoped they would give him some respite from the silliness at Jordan Court.

His plan had been working well, for he had taken meals with his brother's guests and, after, had excused himself to find a quiet place for his studies. Then everything had changed when he was introduced to Miss Primrose Dunsworthy. He had learned of her interest in the baffling hieroglyphics, and he had offered her the chance to read his favorite books on the topic. She had gleefully accepted, expressing her gratitude with more words than he had heard her speak during the rest of her stay at Jordan Court.

She had returned to her home and he to his. He hoped she had found more serenity than he had in the advent of the wedding at Fortenbury Park. How wonderful it would have been to spend his time with a book! The one time he had been able to steal some time for himself, he had discovered he needed one of the books he had lent Miss Rosie.

But it had not been for the chance to retrieve the book or even to discuss its contents that he had followed Wandersee's carriage to this small village. Why he was here was something he wished to keep to himself just now.

He caught sight of a simple house past a thick

row of trees. Those evergreens must protect the house and its thatched roof from the winds off the sea. He could see very little before the carriage turned in to a road that appeared to lead behind the house.

"Dunsworthy Dower Cottage will seem quite primitive to you, I am sure," Miss Rosie said, her gaze focused on her hands in her lap.

He did not need to see her eyes, for after she had taken her leave from his brother's house, their intriguing green color had lingered like the image imprinted upon his eyes when he stared at the sun. Since he had last spoken with her, he had persuaded himself that he had been mistaken to believe that he had seen an intelligence in those eyes that would challenge his own. He had been wrong to listen to his own doubts.

But who could blame him when other women were so— He refused to finish that thought. He had not ridden such a distance to let the problem that had plagued him at Fortenbury Park fill his every thought. He had come to Dunsworthy Dower Cottage to discover a way to escape them. If Miss Rosie said little, that did not bother him. In fact he appreciated her restraint. Far better a few sensible words instead of a plethora of prattle.

By thunder! He would not think of *her* and all the words she used to batter his ears.

"Your home will seem quite comfortable, Miss Rosie," he said, hoping a conversation with her would banish memories of other, far less pleasing ones. "I look forward to a pleasant house after the coaching inns that have been my hosts for the past two nights."

"Two? We needed to spend only one night in an inn when we traveled to Plymouth."

"I came from Bath."

He could see, beyond the rim of her plain bonnet, her lips tilting. She looked up at him, and he could think of no other description for her smile than dazzling.

"That is right," she said with a light laugh. "I keep thinking that the wedding will be held in Plymouth. I forget that it will be celebrated at your family's seat in Bath."

"You are still planning to attend, I am assuming."

"Yes." She dimpled. "That is why Moss had instructions from Lucian to bring the carriage. Now Aunt Millicent and I can travel in style to your brother's wedding."

The carriage rolled to a stop, and Rupert opened the door before Moss could come around. Jumping out, he was pleased that the coachman had halted the carriage away from one of the numerous puddles dotting the stableyard. Tracking mud into the Dunsworthy home would be beyond rude. The rain was almost over. The heaviest clouds were vanishing to the east, so there should be no more storms tonight, but an early autumnal chill was settling around them.

"Hand me your baskets, Miss Rosie," he said, giving himself a chance to appraise the cottage as he took the baskets and placed them on the low stone wall edging the stableyard.

The wall that was stained from centuries of spray from the sea also surrounded what was, he discovered, the remnants of a kitchen garden. He looked beyond the withering vines and plants to the back of the house. It was a twin in appearance to the front. Despite the thatched roof lowering over the door like heavy brows, the back door looked as cozy as the front. Mayhap it was the small well set in the very center of the kitchen garden or it might have been the bucket holding the last flowers of the season. It was not a pretentious house for it did not have aspirations of being as grand as Fortenbury Park or Dunsworthy Hall, Miss Rosie's cousin's manor house. Yet, he suspected he would be very comfortable within the cottage's walls.

Turning back to the carriage, he reached up to hand Rosie out just as he heard a voice call, "Moss, we did not expect you for another week!"

Rupert did not need Rosie's murmur of "Aunt Millicent" to recognize the cheerful voice. He had been astonished to discover that Millicent Dunsworthy was Rosie's aunt and not a third Dunsworthy sister. Barely a decade separated Millicent in age from Rosie's older sister, Bianca. Her hair, even though it was drawn back, appeared to be made of spun gold, and her blue eyes had the same aura of intellect as her niece's.

Miss Dunsworthy pushed open the gate that separated the kitchen garden from the stableyard. She was wiping her hands on a gray apron she wore over a pink sprigged gown. When she saw him, she halted in midstep.

"Lord Fortenbury, what a delightful surprise!" Miss Dunsworthy smiled, and he knew, in spite of what must be astonishment at seeing him, her smile was sincere. "I had thought you would be quite busy in Bath just now."

"Miss Dunsworthy, when I learned Moss was bringing Wandersee's carriage to Dunstanbury, I could not resist following. After all, only a foolish man would resist any opportunity to call on you."

He bowed over Miss Dunsworthy's hand and returned her smile, hoping that Moss would not step forward to hand Miss Rosie out of the carriage. It was a pleasure he wanted to reserve for himself.

"And to avoid the myriad preparations for your brother's wedding."

"Yes, you understand my plight very well." Why hadn't he thought of such an excuse himself? That would have allowed him to give Miss Rosie the answer she desired and put a quick end to her obvious curiosity.

Holding up his hand, he grinned as Miss Rosie placed her slender fingers on it. By thunder! She was betwattling him again as she had before, distracting him as he had dared to hope from the problem that had sent him after Wandersee's carriage.

She withdrew her fingers from his grip as soon as she stood on the ground, but gave him a smile while she thanked him. Her aunt was correct. He had come here, in part, to get away from the wedding arrangements. Not just his brother's, but the constant discussion of matches made and marriages celebrated and heirs produced. Each discussion had been aimed, it seemed, at the question of why his younger brother was marrying before Rupert did. The obligation as he had been reminded again and again—as if he could forget it—was his to produce an heir to the respected title that had become his upon his father's death.

Miss Dunsworthy patted his arm, drawing his thoughts back to her. "You have my sympathies, my lord. It was our good fortune that Rosie's sister, Bianca, wished to have a quiet and quick wedding."

"Which surprised many among the *ton*."

"It should not take long for the *ton* to learn that

Bianca always does what she thinks is right, no matter what anyone else thinks."

"An admirable trait," he replied.

Miss Rosie rolled her eyes. "Not necessarily."

"No?" He wanted to keep her talking, and she seemed more relaxed here in the drenched stableyard than he had ever seen her. "I can assume that it is not easy to live with someone who is certain that she is always right. Is your sister usually right?"

"*That* is why she can prove to be bothersome. She almost always is right."

Rupert laughed as he had not in longer than he could recall. There was something so earnest and honest about Rosie Dunsworthy. Was that why he had not been able to get her out of his thoughts since they last had spoken? As he admired her ruddy hair and her eyes, which were now the exact shade of fresh grass, he knew he must be as honest as she was. It was not just her sincerity that had pushed her again and again into his mind. Those demure eyes sparkled with just a hint of deviltry when she thought no one was looking. They had intrigued him as much as her beguiling curves.

"I would find that most bothersome as well," he said before turning to Miss Dunsworthy. "Your niece has assured me that I am not imposing by seeking your hospitality tonight."

Miss Dunsworthy's eyes glistened as brightly as Miss Rosie's. "We welcome the chance to return your family's kindnesses to us, my lord. Your brother has been our generous host, and soon you shall be hosting us as well. We are delighted to have the chance to make you at home beneath our roof."

"Miss Rosie has assured me as well that you have a feast prepared for us tonight."

"A feast?" Her smile wavered.

Miss Rosie chuckled. "Aunt Millicent, he is speaking of the bread you made this morning and"—she flipped back the cloth on the smaller basket—"Mrs. Hanover's preserves."

Rupert watched, amused, as Miss Dunsworthy gave Miss Rosie an enthusiastic hug. Even if he had never met these two ladies before this very moment, he would know by their actions that theirs was a home filled with happiness and love.

He looked inland and saw the distant shape of Dunsworthy Hall. Until the death of Miss Rosie's brother in the war against Napoleon, the family had resided there as their ancestors had for generations before them. Now Miss Rosie's cousin had the title and the estate, and the ladies had been exiled here to the dower cottage. Had it been, he wondered, a self-imposed exile? The infrequent conversations he had had with the present Lord Dunsworthy had left him with an unsatisfactory impression. The man was too sure of himself and his opinions, much as Miss Rosie's older sister, but Rupert recalled with a silent chuckle, he had found *her* charming.

"Moss, you will join us for supper, too, won't you?" Miss Dunsworthy was asking as the coachman came out of the barn.

Rupert had failed to notice the coachee unhooking the horses from the carriage and taking them into the barn. His brother would have chuckled, reminding Rupert how much he missed while immersed in his studies.

When Moss glanced at him, uneasy, Miss Dunsworthy laughed. "One of the good things about not being an actual part of the *ton* is that we are not bound by its strictures. Here, in Dunsworthy Dower Cottage, kings and scullery maids are both welcome to dine at the same table."

"Aunt Millicent!" Rosie was astounded at how her aunt spoke with Lord Fortenbury. Aunt Millicent usually followed the rules of the Polite World, even within their small cottage.

Her aunt wagged a finger at her. "Do not put me to the scold, young lady." Without giving Rosie a chance to answer, she picked up the two baskets and added to Moss, "Come in and have a cup of something warm while you tell me the latest tidings from Wandersee Manor. I am certain I shall have many questions, so that you will need both tea and supper to answer them all."

Rosie smiled, understanding why Aunt Millicent had invited Moss to dine at the same table as Lord Fortenbury. Her aunt missed Bianca. As did Rosie. It had been such a short time since the wedding, but it seemed that Bianca had been gone for too long. Bianca had promised to try to return from her honeymoon in time to attend Lord Fortenbury's brother's wedding. Rosie hoped that would be possible.

As Moss, who insisted on carrying the baskets, went with Aunt Millicent, who was already peppering him with questions, Rosie glanced at Lord Fortenbury. She took a deep breath, wanting to keep the words from becoming stuck in her throat again.

"If you want to bring your things," she said, "I can show you where the guest room is. I hope you do not find it too primitive."

"The guest room is beneath the eaves of your cozy cottage, as I recall from Lucian's tales of his first visit here."

"It is directly beneath the roof." Her smile grew wider, and she was thrilled that the viscount still was as easy to speak with as he had been in Plymouth. "I fear you will find the ceiling far lower than your liking, my lord, for it slants almost to the floor."

"You will find that I am not planning to spend much time there. I had hoped to have time to discuss with you what you have read, and I doubt your aunt, in spite of her democratic invitation to dinner, would be open-minded enough to allow us to have that conversation in my bedchamber."

"You doubt correctly."

He chuckled under his breath as he opened the carriage's boot and drew out a small satchel. "Lead on, Miss Rosie."

Wanting to motion for him to go first through the gate to the kitchen garden so his eyes were not aimed at her back and watching every motion, Rosie told herself not to be rude. How many times had Bianca chided her for being shy? Bianca would have been amazed to hear how much Rosie had spoken to Lord Fortenbury when they met in the village, because Rosie was too often tongue-tied with people beyond her family.

*A good hostess always goes out of her way to make a guest comfortable.* Aunt Millicent's voice played through her head, reminding Rosie of the obligations she had. Not that Rosie forgot them; she just hoped she could fulfill them. Before Bianca was married, Rosie could always depend on her sister to keep the silence from becoming too oppressive. Now . . .

"Please watch where you step," Rosie said.

"I see that there are puddles everywhere." His answer came from very close behind her. She had not expected him to follow on her heels.

"I meant watch out for the chickens. They will run underfoot in an effort to escape."

He laughed. "Brainless birds."

She was glad she did not have to reply. She hurried through the kitchen garden that was almost dead. Most of the vegetables and herbs had been picked earlier in the month. The vegetables were in the root cellar or bottled and on the shelf in the larder. The herbs had been bunched and hung from every rafter in the kitchen, drying and adding to the fragrance of whatever was baked each day. Now the chickens were gleaning what remained.

Aunt Millicent barely took her gaze from Moss's face as Rosie led Lord Fortenbury through the kitchen, which was filled with the aroma of freshly baked bread. After their guests were settled, Aunt Millicent would share the tidings with her.

"This is, indeed, charming," Lord Fortenbury said as they walked into the sitting room. "Not at all primitive."

Rosie looked at the settee, which was showing signs of wear in spite of the blanket covering the most threadbare areas. Two out of the three chairs were claimed by cats. Barley, the family's dog, must still be on the upstairs landing, where, on sunny days, light heated the floor during the afternoon. Later, he would assume his spot beside the hearth, hoping a fire would be lit. A single table was placed in front of the settee, and a lamp sat precariously on the wide sill of a window looking toward the sea. Aunt Millicent called it their "wanderer's light," for it would be a beacon to anyone who passed the house in search of shelter.

"Thank you," Rosie remembered to say. The bashfulness was returning double-fold, but she had no idea how to shove it aside. Having Lord Fortenbury here in the cottage was something that unsettled her, and she had no idea why. She had enjoyed speaking with him at Jordan Court and in the village. Even in the yard, words had come facilely. Yet, here in the cottage's main room, she was ill at ease. Somehow she managed to say, "Please come this way."

She heard his footsteps close behind her—*very* close behind her again—as she walked out into the entry hall. It was not wide, and the staircase took much of the space. Crossing the recently cleaned stone floor, she put her hand on the newel post.

"Be certain to duck, my lord," she said as she recalled the low overhang near the middle of the shadowed stairs.

"I shall. Thank you for the warning."

Climbing the steps, she paused to pat Barley's head where he was lying in the remnants of the sunlight coming through the thinning clouds. She gasped when Lord Fortenbury's bag bumped into her.

"Forgive me," he said quickly. "I did not notice that you had stopped."

"My fault."

"What do we have here?" He bent to look at Barley, who was regarding him with an open-mouthed grin. Patting the brown patch on Barley's black forehead, he said, "I see you have an excellent guard to protect this family."

"He barks whenever anyone comes to the front door. As you are already within, he must assume you present no danger to us."

"An excellent guard and quite wise. You are lucky to have such a fine beast."

"Or it may be simply that he is too lazy to move

when he is trying to let any hint of today's rare sunshine heat his coat." She smiled when Barley wagged his tail as if he understood her words.

Lord Fortenbury laughed, and she wondered if he had any idea how infectious the sound was. Such a genuine laugh, unreserved and unaffected, sent musical notes racing through her head. She tried to match the notes to the sound of that laughter but was able to capture only a few.

"That simply proves my statement that he is an intelligent beast," he said. "I have heard it said that beasts often reflect the manners of their owners." He chuckled again. "Not that I am suggesting that you are idle. Rather, that you are sagacious."

Rosie hated the blush that seared her cheeks, but she could not halt it. Any attempts to do so made the color brighter. Hoping the light was dreary enough so Lord Fortenbury would not see her scarlet cheeks, she hurried along the upper corridor.

She opened the door to what was, now that Bianca was wed, the extra bedroom. It was even simpler than the sitting room downstairs. A bed topped by a white coverlet was set under the slanting ceiling. Beside the single window, a table held a pitcher and a bowl. A braided rug in front of the raised hearth had been downstairs until it became ragged and was banished up here.

"I was correct," Lord Fortenbury said as he placed his bag on the rug. "This is far nicer than the rooms I have rented for the past two nights." He started to turn, then yelped as he bumped his head on the ceiling.

"My lord—"

"No need to apologize. You warned me to be cautious. 'Tis not your fault that I was unthinking."

Rosie locked her fingers together behind her. "If you wish to clean the dust from the road off you, I can bring up some water."

"I did not seek your hospitality so you could act as a servant in your own home."

"We are your hosts. It is meet that I see to each of your needs."

The abrupt heat on her cheeks struck her like a blow as Lord Fortenbury smiled at her unfortunate choice of words. She wanted to dress him down for that smile. If he had pretended not to hear a secondary meaning, she might not be blushing fiercely now. She could not blame him for her own words.

"Miss Rosie, you are very kind, but I shall bring up water myself after supper."

"If you insist."

"I do."

She nodded, eager to escape before she humiliated herself further. "If you need anything to make you more comfortable, my lord, be sure to speak to me of it."

"If I need any*thing* to make me comfortable, I shall let you know."

She did not wait to listen to what else he might have to stay. She had made enough of a fool of herself. Hurrying to leave the room, along the hall, and down the stairs, she went out the front door. She wanted to keep Aunt Millicent and Moss from seeing her crimsom cheeks. Somehow, she was going to have to find a way to govern her blushing before she went to Fortenbury Park and the wedding. She wished she knew how.

# CHAPTER THREE

Leaning back in his chair, Rupert put his napkin beside his plate, which was empty save for a few bread crumbs. He looked around the table. Miss Dunsworthy was stirring her tea and Moss was dipping his knife into the nearly empty jar of preserves. They had kept up a steady conversation throughout the meal, but Miss Rosie had not uttered a single word. Each time Rupert had glanced in her direction, she had quickly lowered her gaze.

By thunder! He had not intended to disconcert her with his teasing comment. The words had meant no more than he had said, exactly as hers had not had a true hidden meaning. But he had neglected to recall that Miss Rosie had never been a part of a Season in London, where words, in addition to being part of a pleasant conversation, could be used as either a weapon or a tool to get what one wished. If she remained as mute during the whole of his call, he would not have the chance to discuss with her the archaeology books he had lent her. *And you won't be able to escape the bothersome thoughts that brought you here.* Mayhap he should be grateful for her protracted silence. If she did not talk to him, there was no chance he could betray the truth of why he had taken off after Wandersee's carriage like a knight of the pad chasing down his prey.

His right hand fisted on his leg. Was he more concerned that Miss Rosie would discover the truth about why he had left Fortenbury Park than he was about her wounded sensibilities? A most ungentlemanly way to think, but avoiding the truth would gain him nothing. A country miss like Rosie Dunsworthy could not guess that he had left his own home in the middle of the night to avoid being caught in the parson's mousetrap as his brother was. He doubted if Miss Rosie had ever met anyone like Ophelia King, who had targeted him and his title and had set off on her own personal crusade to possess both.

"That sounds just like Lucian," said Miss Dunsworthy, her laughter freeing Rupert from those uncomfortable thoughts. She lifted a platter that held a last piece of bread. "Would you like to finish this, my lord?"

"I fear I am not up to the task. Moss?"

The coachman nodded. "Thank you, my lord. I think I am quite capable of eating another piece of this wonderful bread and the delicious preserves." He rubbed his stomach as he grinned. "Don't let Cook at Wandersee Manor ever learn that I said this, Miss Dunsworthy, but she could take some baking lessons from you."

"You could start a revolt within the walls of Wandersee Manor with such talk," Rupert said. "However, I must second Moss's comments, Miss Dunsworthy. This is the best meal I have had in longer than I can remember. Unlike Moss, however, I implore you to repeat those words to the cook at Fortenbury Park so she realizes that she would be wise to recall how simple fare like this is often the tastiest."

Miss Dunsworthy blushed almost as brightly as her niece had earlier. "You are too kind, my lord."

"I assure you that my compliments are sincere. I cannot recall when I have had such pleasant-tasting preserves and soft bread."

"Then we must be certain to bring you several jars of Mrs. Hanover's best fruit preserves when we come to Fortenbury Park for your brother's wedding." Miss Dunsworthy smiled and changed the course of the conversation by asking, "How is Mr. Jordan?"

"Nervous." He laughed again, relaxing against his chair. "As the day approaches, he acts more and more like a conveyancer on his way to face the hangman."

"He seemed jovial when we saw him in Plymouth."

He stretched and picked up a bottle of wine from a shelf by the dry sink. "Henry has found that keeping this close tends to erode the edges of his anxiety over his pending nuptials. He is determined to have everything just perfect for his fiancée. Perfection has never been an issue for him before, and he is ill-equipped to deal with how the more he tries, the more he fails to achieve that ideal he has set for himself."

He was taken aback when Miss Rosie smiled and said, "I am endlessly amazed how men seem to dread the wedding ceremony when they are the ones who propose marriage in the first place."

"In the *first* place," he said, leaning his elbows on the table as he caught her eyes, determined not to let them escape him again, "a man may offer a proposal of marriage. However, I have spoken with many gentlemen who assure me that they found themselves making that offer simply because it seemed the proper thing to do when the lady had turned the discussion in that direction."

"And in the second place?"

"Matchmaking mamas and papas had made many less than subtle hints that such an offer was long overdue."

"So you wish us to believe that men propose marriage only because they are cornered into it?" She laughed. When her aunt did, too, she glanced at Miss Dunsworthy.

He kept his smile in place, in spite of Miss Rosie's obvious attempt to avoid his gaze. He could not mention it when anyone else who was not watching her closely would have seen the motion as very commonplace. "Being cornered into making an offer may be the only way out of a young miss's trap is what Henry assures me whenever he is deep in his cups."

Miss Dunsworthy shook her head. "I am of the mind this is a myth perpetuated by men who do not wish to own that love is the reason that they wish to marry."

"Save for those who wed for money."

"A very different situation." She smiled broadly. "Those grooms very nearly dance to the altar."

"Aunt Millicent!" gasped Miss Rosie.

"Do not chide me when I am speaking the truth, Rosie."

Laughing, Miss Rosie said, "You are not usually cynical."

"True, but Lord Fortenbury was being honest; I felt I must be the same."

"I fear," Rupert said, "I bring out the worst in all of you."

Rosie let her aunt reassure Lord Fortenbury that his comments were both entertaining and thought-provoking. Looking down at the half-slice of bread still on her plate, Rosie did not want to own that the viscount had been quite accurate about her when he said he brought out the very worst reactions from each of them. Every word he spoke seemed to create the most inappropriate thoughts in her head.

When Aunt Millicent offered to serve a very special dessert—a delicious strawberry tart—in the sitting room, Rosie said, "Go ahead, Aunt Millicent. You have spent the day baking. I will bring it in for you and our guests."

"Thank you." She pushed back her chair. "Will you join me, gentlemen?"

Moss glanced toward the door. "I need to check the carriage before dark. The back right wheel seemed a bit loose."

"I will bring your dessert out to you," Rosie said.

"You are very kind, Miss Rosie. If you would give me an hour to do my work, I would be grateful." He walked out of the kitchen, carrying with him the last slice of bread with a generous serving of preserves atop it.

Aunt Millicent took the teapot from where it was being kept warm on the kitchen hearth and carried it into the sitting room. Going to the oven built in the side of the fireplace, Rosie drew open the door, which had been partly ajar. She found a cloth to protect her hands and lifted out the tart.

"That smells wonderful."

Lord Fortenbury's voice was too close. How was he able to get so near without her being aware of him? She fought not to drop the tart as her hands trembled. When she turned to carry it to the table, he stepped aside to let her pass.

"Aunt Millicent is, as you have already found out for yourself, an excellent cook."

"Did she make this?"

Rosie looked over her shoulder. "No."

"I thought not from how she described it as an exceptional dessert." He drew in a deep breath and smiled. "And I assume this was not prepared by the talented Mrs. Hanover."

"No."

"Then you must have baked this."

"How did you know?"

He shrugged. "I could say it was a lucky guess only, but it was not. In addition to the pride in your aunt's voice when she announced the dessert, I recalled you mentioning that your aunt was baking bread, but you said nothing of this delicious-smelling dessert that you must have made before you went into the village."

"Do you watch everyone as closely as you have us?"

"Sometimes, when the people are intriguing."

"So you can see the worst you bring out in people?"

He laughed as she cut servings of the strawberry tart. "I had not guessed I bring out the worst in you. I would have said rather that I have brought out the best in you."

"The best? I do not like to think that my behavior this evening has been my best."

"But you have said more, save during supper, than I have ever heard you speak."

"You barely know me."

"Now." He picked up one of the small plates where she had placed pieces of tart. "But I suspect we shall become much better acquainted during my visit here and your visit to Fortenbury Park."

"You sound very assured of that, my lord."

"I am."

Rosie decided it would be wise not to answer what sounded like a challenge. Reaching for the other two plates, she pulled back when Lord Fortenbury picked up another. Their fingers brushed, and she looked hastily away. She had been certain that the powerful sensations she had experienced while dancing with him at Jordan Court had been because of the excitement of the music and the crowded room.

Now the same melody was swelling through her head, a song that seemed to have no pattern she could discern. It was a tapestry of the first trill of a spring bird and the cacophony of a thunderstorm and the heated whisper of a summer wind. She had heard its like only once before . . . when she was in Lord Fortenbury's arms dancing.

"Is there something wrong?" he asked as he turned toward the sitting room. "Letting this tart grow cold would be a waste."

"Y-y-yes," she managed to stutter. How could he be unaware of the powerful music that was both within her and lilting across her skin?

Rosie put the rest of the tart back in the oven to stay warm, then took the last plate in to where Aunt Millicent was shooing the cats off the chairs. Her aunt gave her a curious glance, and Rosie wondered what her face was divulging. It did not feel as hot as when she blushed, so there must be something else. She wished she could ask what her aunt was seeing, because Lord Fortenbury was certain to see it as well.

Sitting on the settee across from her aunt, Rosie watched the viscount start to sit on the other chair. Her cry of warning was drowned out by a cat's yowl.

"Pay her no mind," Aunt Millicent said. "She always sneaks back onto a chair, even when we try to persuade her to get down. You can shove her off the chair."

Lord Fortenbury smiled. "And risk getting cat hair all over my tart? I would rather not." He looked back at Rosie. "May I join you on the settee, Miss Rosie?"

"Yes." What else could she say? That she would take the chair and leave the whole settee to him? Such an answer would be beyond rude.

As Aunt Millicent asked Lord Fortenbury about his journey from Bath, Rosie was glad to let the conversation waft around her. Her aunt glanced at her several times, and Rosie knew Aunt Millicent wanted her to participate in the conversation. She would if she had something to say that she could get past her stiff lips.

How she wished she could participate in the give and take of commonplaces with the ease of her aunt and Lord Fortenbury! Not that anything he said sounded practiced. Quite to the contrary, for he seemed eager to hear her aunt's response to each comment he made.

"You should ask Rosie about that," Aunt Millicent said.

"Then I shall," he replied with a smile. Shifting slightly so he could look at her, he asked, "What do you think, Miss Rosie?"

About what? She had been watching how they spoke with such apparent ease; she had not paid any attention to what they were saying. She must say something. Aunt Millicent would be horrified if she continued to sit there as mute as a stone.

A knock came from the front door, and Rosie breathed a sigh of relief. The wrong thing to do, she realized as both her aunt and the viscount regarded her with bafflement.

"I wonder who that could be," Aunt Millicent said as she stood.

Lord Fortenbury came to his feet, but she motioned for him to return to his seat as she went out of the room. He sat as Barley bounded down the stairs, barking.

"Do callers always create chaos in your house?" he asked, sitting again beside her.

"Usually."

He cut another bite from his tart and smiled. "I trust my arrival did not create chaos like this."

"No! Aunt Millicent was pleased to see you. Do you doubt her assertion?"

"And you? Were you pleased to see me?"

"Are you in such great need for reassurance, my lord, that you must ask about it again and again?" She stared down at her tart when his eyes widened at her sharp question.

"Forgive me, Miss Rosie."

"Yes."

When she said nothing more, she thought he would continue eating his tart. She hoped it was more appealing to him and Aunt Millicent than it was to her. She placed her fork on the plate on her lap. She found each bite more difficult than the previous one, for the fragrant tart turned to dry dust on her tongue.

His finger under her chin tilted her face up. Shocked at his bold action, she stared up at his dark eyes.

"I trust," he said, "you will be honest with me here as you were at Jordan Court. If I have done anything to distress you, please say so."

"There is nothing."

His finger stroked her jaw, and an odd buzzing

filled her head. No, not a buzzing, but a rapid pulse that rushed through her like a spring tide. The slightest hint of a smile touched his lips. Did he know about her odd reaction to his touch, or could he feel it as well?

"I know, Miss Rosie, you do not like to air your opinions like a gabble grinder. However, at Jordan Court, you did not bring a conversation to a halt with a single-word answer." He leaned toward her. "If I have done something to vex you, you need only say so."

*Yes, you vex me. You discompose me with your touch. You create feelings in me that I don't understand.* The words burst into her mouth, but she refused to let them past her lips. She almost laughed at the irony. Often she had tried to force an answer out; now she was trying to withhold it.

"Right this way." Aunt Millicent came back into the room. "We were just enjoying—oh, my!"

At her aunt's dismay, Rosie pulled away from Lord Fortenbury. She looked at Aunt Millicent and saw her aunt was not alone. Next to her was Constable Powers. The constable was dressed in his very best dark brown coat, and his scuffed shoes were polished to the highest sheen possible for old leather. He even was wearing the light blue waistcoat he wore only when he stood before the justice of the peace to present a case against some miscreant. His face was frozen in a macabre caricature of a smile. Even that fell away as he scowled at her.

Lord Fortenbury set himself on his feet, and the motion was enough to jar her plate from her knees. It dropped to the floor with a crash of broken china and the clatter of the fork bouncing under the settee. The cats pounced on the tart, eager for an unexpected treat. Barley stuck his nose between them, for he did not want to be left out.

"Good evening, constable," Lord Fortenbury said as calmly as if he stood in the middle of a reception line rather than a disaster.

"My lord." Constable Powers gave the merest bow of his head, and his scowl became even more furious.

"I trust you have not come to let me know I have inadvertently broken the law again."

"No, my lord." His voice was colder than she had ever heard. "I had not guessed you would still be here."

"Miss Dunsworthy and her niece have been gracious enough to act as my hosts." He smiled at them. "My hostesses, I should say."

Even under the trying circumstances, Rosie found his smile pleasant. Too pleasant, she feared, because that same flutter of her pulse flew through her again.

The flutter froze when Lord Fortenbury said, "If I am intruding on your call on these ladies, I can ask you to excuse me."

Constable Powers's eyes lit up for a moment with satisfaction, but before he could speak, Aunt Millicent said, "Nonsense, my lord. What is it they say? The more, the merrier. Then we shall be a merry group this evening."

"You are always gracious, Miss Dunsworthy." Lord Fortenbury's smile grew wider, but he glanced at Constable Powers.

The constable's color rose again as he stuttered out, "Th-th-thank you for your w-w-welcome, Miss Dunsworthy."

Rosie wanted to offer her sympathy to Constable Powers, because she comprehended all too well how difficult it was to find the right thing to say when everyone was looking at one and expecting an answer. She opened her mouth to say something, then realized she had nothing to say that would not add to the tension in the room.

"Rosie," Aunt Millicent said quietly, "please bring some of your tart for Constable Powers while I clean up this mess."

"I can—"

Her aunt interrupted her in a tone almost as honed as the one Constable Powers had used. "Go into the kitchen while I clean up this mess."

Rosie nodded and went to the door. She paused and looked back over her shoulder. Had her aunt meant the ruined tart on the floor or the tautness between Lord Fortenbury and Constable Powers? She could not loiter in the doorway to discover the answer.

Her knees were trembling when she reached into the oven and drew out the tart. Making sure there would be enough left for Moss, she cut another piece. For a moment, she considered taking the coachman's dessert out to him in the barn. If she stayed there, listening to the tales of his journeys while working for the Wandersee family, she would not have to face what waited in the sitting room.

She frowned. What *did* wait there? She could not doubt the antagonism between Lord Fortenbury and Constable Powers. Was it more than the fact that Constable Powers had scolded Lord Fortenbury for the rapid speed of the carriage coming into Dunstanbury?

Rosie made sure she had a smile on her face when she walked back into the sitting room. When Lord Fortenbury came to his feet, Constable Powers popped up like a marionette whose strings had been tugged. She was aware of every eye in the room being focused on her as she handed Constable Powers the plate.

"You will find it very tasty," Lord Fortenbury said in an obvious effort to ease the discomfort.

"I am well-familiar with Miss Rosie's fine desserts."

"Then do not let me delay you from enjoying this one."

"I will enjoy what Miss Rosie has offered me. I always do." The constable flushed almost to the shade of the strawberries on the plate.

Rosie wanted to find the words to assure Constable Powers he had said nothing worthy of such a blush. Then she saw Aunt Millicent's face bleaching, and she repeated the constable's words again in her mind. Her eyes widened as she realized the secondary meaning they could have. Such words could be the ruin of a young woman.

Constable Powers must have known that, too, because he said in a choked voice, "Forgive me, Miss Rosie. I would never suggest anything . . . anything . . ."

"Anything that would blemish her reputation," Lord Fortenbury said quietly.

"That is it exactly." The constable put the plate with its untouched tart on the table and clasped his hands behind his back. "Miss Rosie, please accept my deepest apology."

"Yes," she said as she had when Lord Fortenbury spoke almost the same words. She took a step back from the others, then another. "Moss is waiting for his dessert. Excuse me."

She had to fight her feet, which wanted to flee at their top speed. Going out into the kitchen, she put the last serving of the tart on a plate and went out into the kitchen garden. She drew in a deep breath, relieved to have escaped the mortifying events in the sitting room. She never had been ill at ease with Constable Powers . . . except this afternoon on the church steps in Dunstanbury. Both times, Lord Fortenbury had been present, making her too aware of how oddly she reacted each time the viscount was near. When she had been in Lord Fortenbury's arms, dancing to a waltz, she had thrilled to the excitement of what seemed like one of the stories her sister used to tell by the hearth. Anything was possible within such a tale. She knew it could not be like that when reality surrounded her instead of perfumed ladies and well-dressed gentlemen. She was shy Primrose Dunsworthy, who would not say shoo to a goose, not some elegant lady who expected the men to pledge their honor and even their lives in exchange for a smile from her.

Yet she was thrilled each time Lord Fortenbury smiled or spoke to her. His touch, chaste though it had been, had delighted her even more. She had reveled in the fairy tale at Jordan Court. She must not let herself believe it could continue at Dunsworthy Dower Cottage or at Fortenbury Park. If she did, she could say the worst possible thing, or she could find it impossible to answer any question from the other guests.

Then Lord Fortenbury would deem her as silly as that goose. That was the most uncomfortable thought of all.

# CHAPTER FOUR

Taking Moss's dessert out to the stable was sure to bring the relief Rosie had hoped for. The quiet within the barn always offered her a respite because the animals did not care if she chattered like a prattle-box or was silent.

But she looked back at the cottage. Guilt taunted her because she had left Aunt Millicent to deal with the two men. Her aunt was capable of mediating such tension and more, but abandoning her to the task left a peculiar taste in Rosie's mouth that had nothing to do with the strawberries.

Why was Lord Fortenbury acting strangely? At his brother's house, he had been pleasing company, eager to talk about the very things that intrigued her—the recent discoveries in Egypt and the strange language used by the ancient pharaohs. Tonight he had acted as if he wanted to share a very different intrigue with her. Had she been completely misled by his charm at Jordan Court? She almost laughed. Charm was what he was trying to use on her now to betwattle her.

She had not expected him to use every opportunity to discuss matters that had nothing to do with the subjects of the books she had borrowed. Those books had been written about the ancient world along the Nile. Since the battles against Napoleon in Egypt, interest in the distant past had grown. She had been most fascinated with the picture writing of the pharaohs.

How silly she had been to think that Lord Fortenbury was truly interested in such an erudite conversation! He seemed to be intent on engaging her in a flirtation. She was tempted to tell him not to waste his fascinating arts on her. There must be plenty of females in the Polite World who would welcome his attentions.

Rosie paused by where Moss was polishing the wheels of the carriage. "Here is your dessert."

He looked up and grinned. "Has it been an hour already?"

"I thought you would want the tart before it dried out too much in the oven," she said, not wanting to own to the truth of how little time had actually passed.

Taking the plate, he leaned back against the carriage. "Between you and your aunt," he said, taking a bite, "this cottage has the best food in this part of England."

"I am pleased that you like it." She must have given herself away more than she had realized, because the coachee knew she had cooked this dessert. How had that happened?

She let her shoulders relax when Moss answered, "Tell your aunt that I shall be looking for more excuses to come and sample her cooking."

Moss had not guessed that she had made the dessert. She was letting her own disquiet color everything around her. And why did it matter so dashed much that Lord Fortenbury had discerned the truth?

Mayhap because everything was not going as she had expected when she next spoke with the viscount. She had looked forward to talking with him since leaving his brother's house almost a month ago. While she had read the books, she had been curious about his opinions on the authors' statements. Now instead of relishing this chance to speak with him, she was acting silly, running away like a child who wanted to avoid getting scolded by her elders.

"Miss Rosie?" called a male voice from the other side of the carriage. It was muffled, so she could not guess who was speaking.

A twinge cut through her when she saw Constable Powers standing on the far side of the wall. The frown he had worn in the sitting room was still tightening his lips.

He waited until she stood beside him before saying in a near whisper, "I must speak with you."

"About what?"

That had been the wrong thing to say, because his frown became even more furious. "You do not need to play coy with me, Miss Rosie."

"I am not."

"You know I am dismayed to have that man acting as if he is your lord and master."

She stared at him in astonishment. A laugh burst from her. Clamping her hand over her mouth, she knew it was too late. Constable Powers was enraged, and her inadvertent laugh had only angered him more.

Lowering her hand, she said, "Constable Powers, you are fretting about something that is not so."

"I saw how you jumped to his orders."

"Aunt Millicent's orders! Aunt Millicent was the one who asked me to bring you some dessert. Aunt Millicent was the one who told me not to clean up the tart from the floor."

His mouth worked, and she knew he was struggling with what he wanted to say. She had seen him wear a similar expression before. Each time it had been when he was trying not to say what he really wished he could.

"Spit it out," she ordered, abruptly as vexed with him as with Lord Fortenbury. If she had not seen Moss's calm kindness, she would have guessed some strange affliction had attacked every man in the shire, turning otherwise sane men into babbling fools.

"He is overly brazen with you!" Color flashed up his cheeks, and she guessed he had not wanted to be so straightforward.

"Constable Powers, you misunderstand—"

"What is there to misunderstand when you let him stroke your face while you gaze up into his eyes?"

Rosie looked away. She should have persuaded Constable Powers long ago that she wished no more than friendship from him. She had tried to be honest with him, but he had persisted, believing that if he lingered nearby she would come to see the good sense in becoming his wife. Mayhap she should have been more forthright, telling him that she wanted the love that appeared in her sister's stories, the love Bianca had found when she was least expecting to.

"I understand," Constable Powers said when she remained silent.

"You do?" She stared at him, again amazed. She

almost asked him to explain to her, because she most certainly did not understand.

He grasped her by the arms and pressed his lips to hers. Before she could react, he released her. He opened his mouth to say something, then spun on his heel and rushed along the road back in the direction of Dunstanbury.

Rosie put her fingers to her lips as she watched him leave. She had thought there would be more to her first kiss, but she had felt nothing but surprise.

"Miss Rosie?"

She whirled, recognizing Lord Fortenbury's voice. Had he seen Constable Powers kiss her? What must he think of her for letting the constable be bold?

He had taken off his coat, and his cravat was loosened. Such undress unnerved her more than Constable Powers's kiss, because it suggested he was completely comfortable at the cottage. Even telling herself that she, as his hostess, should hope he felt that way did nothing to slow her swift heartbeat.

"Did I startle you?" he asked. "Moss said you were over here, and I apologize if you wished to be alone with your thoughts."

Alone? Mayhap he had not seen anything but her standing by the wall and Constable Powers rushing back to the village.

"No." She swallowed roughly, knowing she must not let her shyness overmaster her again. "No, you did not disturb me."

"Good." He smiled. "Do you have some rags that I can use to wrap around Osiris's leg? He seems to be favoring his back right one."

"We keep old rags in a bucket." She walked

around the carriage. "If you tell me what you need, I—"

"I told you that I did not stop here to have you run errands for me." He chuckled and winked at Moss, who laughed, too. "Just tell me where the bucket is."

"Behind the kitchen door."

He tipped an imaginary hat to her. "Thank you, miss."

Moss laughed again quietly as Lord Fortenbury walked toward the kitchen garden. "Some say that viscount has an odd kick in his gallop, but he seems like a *bonhomme* to me. He takes right good care of his mount. Every night, he checks on the horse to be certain it is comfortable before heading off to his own rest."

"How did he come to be traveling with you?" Mayhap Moss would be privy to the information that Lord Fortenbury seemed averse to sharing with her.

"Lord Wandersee sent a message that I was to deliver the wedding gift from him and her ladyship to Fortenbury Park before coming here."

"Oh." She sat on the carriage's step. "I had hoped that they would be attending."

"His lordship told me to let you know that they still plan to be there, but even with the war over, sailing ships seldom keep the schedule set by their masters. A storm that keeps them in port in Italy an extra day or two will prevent them from returning in time for Mr. Jordan's wedding."

Shaking aside her dismals, Rosie asked the question that Lord Fortenbury had avoided answering. "Did the viscount say why he had decided to join you on the trip here?"

"Why are you asking that again? I thought he and your aunt were discussing that when we arrived."

"Yes, yes, they were." Rosie gave him a smile she hoped was not as shaky as it felt.

It must have looked fine, because Moss launched into one of his amusing tales of his travels with the Wandersee family. He soon had her laughing about a misadventure taken by Lucian's mother when they had been halfway to London before the lady realized the invitation had been to a house far to the west in Devon.

Taking the empty plate from Moss, she bid him good night and hurried back to the house before Aunt Millicent began to worry where she might be.

Her aunt was washing dishes by the back door. When Rosie offered to help, Aunt Millicent shook her head.

"We should not leave Lord Fortenbury alone in the sitting room," Aunt Millicent added as she scrubbed a spoon. "That is not being good hosts."

"The sitting room? How did he get there?"

"Through the door and the kitchen." Her aunt set the spoon back into the bucket. "Rosie, you are as jumpy as a highwayman with a constable on his heels. What is amiss?"

Rosie smiled, a genuine smile this time. "Nothing is amiss, Aunt Millicent. I am just amazed that he came out of the barn and I did not see him."

"He did mention that you were in deep conversation with Moss." She gestured with a soapy finger. "The viscount is finishing his dessert in the sitting room. I know you are bursting to talk to him about those Egyptian stones of his, so go and enjoy a nice conversation."

"Constable Powers—"

Her aunt's face clouded for a moment. "His lack of good manners was very unexpected."

"He kissed me, Aunt Millicent." She stared at her feet, wondering why guilt flooded her when *she* had done nothing.

"When?"

"A few minutes ago. Out by the wall."

"Rosie, you should—"

She grasped her aunt's fingers, which were jeweled with soap bubbles. "Do not scold me, Aunt Millicent. I did not give him permission to kiss me."

"Few men ask for permission." She shook her head with a smile. "You have listened to too many of your sister's stories where dashing princes beg the maiden even to hold her hand." Her golden brows lowered. "My dear child, did you give the constable some reason to believe you would welcome his attentions?"

"Not that I recall." She rubbed her hands on her skirt.

"If you have given him a reason, even unwittingly, to believe he has some claim upon your time, Rosie, you need to be honest with him."

"I have tried."

"I suspected as much." She patted Rosie's arm with a soapy hand. "Men often mistake sincerity for coyness."

Rosie gave her aunt a quick smile before turning toward the sitting room door. Coy was the very word Constable Powers had used. Both he and her aunt should know better. Coy was something Rosie could not be. Silent, yes. Shy, yes. Coy, no.

When her aunt shifted on the stoop so that there would be no question of Rosie's being unchaperoned while she spoke with their guest, Rosie's smile became more sincere. She paused in the doorway between the kitchen and the sitting room.

Lord Fortenbury was edged by the soft light from the lamp by the window. He was so tall that his head almost brushed the low ceiling. He had one foot on the edge of the hearth and was staring down at the wood waiting to be lit as the weather turned colder. Even from where she stood, she could see how his gaze was turned inward as if he were far from the cottage.

Something *was* amiss, but not with her. Something, the very thing that had compelled him to leave his estate to come here, was wrong. Twice he had avoided answering her question, so she should not ask him again. He obviously wished to keep the truth to himself.

He must have sensed her staring at him, for he raised his brown eyes, catching her. She did not look away. Her fingers tightened on the door's frame. He seemed to be seeking something in her face. What? His own sternly chiseled features offered no hint of his thoughts.

Then he smiled, transforming his expression from pensive to congenial. "I have been waiting with impatience for you to join me, for this dessert is growing cold."

"You need not have waited for me."

"But how could I share it with you if you were not here?" He gave her a smile that suggested the naughty boy he might have been. "I would have been tempted to eat it all myself if I began."

"It is your dessert."

"As you recall, my own abrupt motion tipped your share off your lap. It is only fair that I share mine with you. If Miss Dunsworthy had not placed our servings by the kitchen hearth, I collect they would have been chilled by now."

"I thought you were still in the barn."

"It took me but a moment to see that Osiris is set for the night." His smile wavered. "A good night's rest should ease the distress on his leg."

"You can trust Moss to look after him."

Motioning for her to sit, he said, "Yes, Moss is an excellent coachee. Just as you and your aunt are excellent hostesses when you welcome me with no forewarning of my visit."

She watched him sit in the chair Aunt Millicent had used before. Relief battled with disappointment within her. Had she lost what good sense she had remaining? She should be glad that Lord Fortenbury was being the gentleman she had expected him to be. Even so, she could not rid her mind of the echo of the sweet song that had soared through her head when he had touched her.

"You said you had read the books I lent you," Lord Fortenbury said, reaching past the gray cat that had climbed into his lap to hand her a plate with half a serving of the tart.

"Yes." At last he wished to speak of the topic they both found fascinating.

"What did you think of the book by Parker, Miss Rosie?"

"I found some of his ideas very simplistic when it comes to understanding the hieroglyphics of ancient Egypt."

"And wrong?"

Rosie set her plate next to his on the table between them. *This* was the way she had hoped their conversation would go from the moment she first greeted him on the village green. "It is not for me to say if he is wrong, my lord."

"But he is. His hypotheses about family life in the royal palace of the pharaohs border on the absurd." He chuckled. "No, I would say they go way beyond absurd."

"He seems very sure of them. He must believe them if he put them in a book for everyone else to read."

"Simply because he had his thoughts published does not mean they have any more validity than anyone else's. I trust you found MacDonald's book more to your taste."

"Professor MacDonald seems to offer more conventional theories that have a greater basis in fact than Mr. Parker."

"Your appraisal matches mine." He smiled. "What did you think of MacDonald's comments on—?" His mouth twisted as he said, "Now, I know there was something I was eager to hear your opinion on. What was it?"

She came to her feet. "If you would like me to get the books, paging through them might help you recall what you wished to discuss with me."

"That would be very pleasant," he said, standing.

"Yes. Please wait here and—"

Barley began barking in the foyer.

Excusing herself, Rosie went to see what was upsetting the dog now. She hoped Constable Powers had not returned, determined to continue their uncomfortable conversation.

"Hush, Barley," she said.

The dog gave her a glance that suggested she was horrible to be unappreciative of his efforts to protect the house. Patting him on the head, she reached for the door.

"Allow me, Miss Rosie," Lord Fortenbury said, his hand covering hers on the latch.

She wanted to draw her hand from beneath his, but she could not move. As she gazed up into his earth-brown eyes, the voice in her head warned her to recall herself faded into a distant whisper. Even her shock that his inadvertent touch elicited a more powerful reaction from her than Constable Powers's kiss drifted into oblivion.

She could only stare up at him. For the first time, she noticed a small scar near his left eye. Curiosity teased her, but she did not ask a question. She let the warmth from his gaze flow over her.

Somewhere, mayhap in her head or mayhap from beyond her, came the strains of a melody she had never heard before. The notes were so soft she doubted she would have noticed them except they provided a song to match the fervid beat of her heart.

His other hand rose to cup her cheek as he leaned toward her, as he had when they were sitting on the settee. Amazement blossomed in his eyes. Was he as much a captive to these unfamiliar sensations as she was? She wanted to put her fingers up to touch his, but again she found it impossible to move. Any word, any action might bring this moment to an abrupt end.

"Barley, what are you barking about now? Oh, my!" Aunt Millicent's reaction was identical to when she had brought Constable Powers into the sitting room.

And so was Lord Fortenbury's. He drew his hands back with obvious reluctance. Clasping them behind him, he said, "We were just about to check outside to discover what had alerted your dog, Miss Dunsworthy."

"Were you?"

Rosie recoiled from her aunt's icy question. Didn't Aunt Millicent trust her to do what was right?

"Yes," Lord Fortenbury replied as he opened the door. When Barley raced past him, he added, "I see some birds near the trees. I believe those birds are what alarmed your dog."

Rosie saw the large birds fleeing before the dog. "Barley loves to chase curlews." She tried to smile. "He waits all summer for them to return to the shore. Doesn't he, Aunt Millicent?"

"Rosie, I believe it is time to retire." Aunt Millicent clearly would not be soothed by any attempts to change the subject. "My lord, I trust your room will be fine for tonight."

"Yes." His shoulders stiffened. "Miss Rosie has already made certain of that, Miss Dunsworthy."

"If you find anything amiss, you are welcome to let *me* know." Aunt Millicent took Rosie's arm and steered her around the viscount. "Good night, my lord."

"Good night." He bowed his head toward them. "And thank you, Miss Rosie, for our interrupted conversation about the various theories expressed in those books."

"You are welcome," she said, not sure what else she could say.

Of one thing she was too painfully certain. Not only did she delight in his touch, but she liked the sound of her name in his deep voice. She liked both far too much.

# CHAPTER FIVE

Rupert was not surprised when Miss Dunsworthy sought him out even before breakfast the next morning. Hearing footfalls as he wiped his face on a towel, he looked up from the well in the kitchen garden to see Miss Dunsworthy wearing the same frown she had last night in the foyer. She had swept Miss Rosie away from him so swiftly he had had no time to explain himself.

"You are leaving today, my lord." She did not make it a question, but he knew it was not truly an order. Miss Dunsworthy would never be ill-mannered.

"You have many preparations before your journey to Fortenbury Park," he replied, falling back on the answer the canons of propriety demanded. "I would be wrong to linger and disrupt them simply because I do not wish to be caught up in the plans at home."

Her mouth twitched, and he knew she was trying not to smile. That she empathized with him was a good sign, for it meant she had not considered him useless as monkey grease in polite society.

"I wish you a good journey, my lord." She paused, then asked, "Where are you bound?"

"To a friend's house." He supposed it was the truth. He did not want to own that he had hoped to impose on Miss Dunsworthy and Miss Rosie a few more nights before he had to return to Fortenbury Park. Now he had to hope someone was lingering in Town. Otherwise, he would have no choice but to go back home. The very idea was appalling.

"Then we shall—"

"My lord!" The shout came from the direction of the stable.

Rupert was amazed to see Moss rushing toward them. As the coachman neared, fury was visible on his face.

"They are gone!" Moss snarled. "Some blasted pad-thief has taken them!"

"What?" asked Miss Dunsworthy. "What are you talking about? What is a pad-thief? What has that pad-thief taken?"

Rupert glanced at her. "A pad-thief is someone who steals horses." Looking back at Moss, he asked, "Are you certain? Could a door have been left open and the horses wandered away?"

"I know better than that, my lord! I always check the door twice before I leave for the night."

"I know you do," he said quickly to apologize for insulting the coachman. Anyone who worked with horses learned, from his earliest days, to make sure the stable door was securely closed when leaving a stable. "I was simply wondering if there could be another way for the door to come open."

Moss nodded. "There was a way. The thief opened it and led the horses out." He flung out a hand toward the barn. "Two thieves, I would venture, by the footprints among the hoofprints."

"You must go for Constable Powers," Miss Dunsworthy said, dismay wiping all other emotion from her face. "He would know if there have been reports of such thievery in the parish. Also you must tell him what has happened so he can be on the alert for your stolen horses."

"I will go." Moss gave them no chance to argue as he rushed out of the kitchen garden.

Rupert frowned. Osiris was a fine horse, and he did not like to think of some thief mistreating him. The chances of getting his horse back were small, for stealing horses was a felony. That meant hanging or transportation. The thieves would be careful not to get caught.

"Constable Powers has been able to stop other thieves," Miss Dunsworthy said, her voice trembling with her alarm. "He has retrieved horses that the thieves have tried to sell at nearby markets."

He looked back at her, and he saw tears filling her eyes. Did she think he would blame *her* for somebody else's felonious acts?

It was difficult to smile, but he forced himself to. "Miss Dunsworthy, that you have faith in the good constable's abilities offers me a great deal of solace."

"I don't know why anyone would come here to take the horses. We have not had other horses in our stable since we moved to the Dower Cottage."

"Our arrival in Dunstanbury was noted by many eyes."

"Are you suggesting someone in Dunstanbury is the thief?" Her blue eyes widened into near-perfect circles.

"I am not accusing anyone, Miss Dunsworthy. I am only stating a fact which was, no doubt, repeated many times in the ensuing hours after our arrival in Dunstanbury. Who knows who might have overheard the tidings of our appearance in the village and how Miss Rosie offered us welcome here? Anyone with malicious intent would be able to determine exactly where the steeds would be."

She nodded and, murmuring something about checking on their breakfast, went into the cottage. He saw her surreptitiously dabbing at her eyes with her apron.

By thunder! The thieves had taken more than the horses. They had stolen Miss Dunsworthy's previously unshakable composure. He hoped if the thieves were captured and brought to trial, the justice of the peace would add that to their list of crimes.

Rupert went to the stable, taking care to step around the many footprints and hoofmarks in the drying mud. Whoever had stolen the horses had not cared that they were leaving a calling card in their wake. Squatting next to several footprints that showed the men had not had an easy time leading all the horses at once, he examined the steps encased in the mud.

Boots, he guessed from the indentations. A cobbler might be able to distinguish his own work, but to Rupert there seemed to be nothing unique about the footprints. He looked back to where his own boots had left their mark in the mud by the well. Except that his heels were tapered to fit into the stirrups, there appeared to be no difference between those prints and these.

He sighed. The theft was the worst ending for a call that had not been what he anticipated when he decided to trail Moss and the carriage from Fortenbury Park. The conversation about hieroglyphics that he had hoped to share with Miss Rosie had lasted for no more than a few words.

*Because you could not stop fantasizing about kissing her!*
He could not argue with the thought that had been his last before he fell asleep last night and his first on awakening this morning. In the days since he had last spoken with Miss Rosie, he had concentrated on recalling her quick mind rather than her soft lips. He had not wanted to think of any lips at all as Ophelia King tried to persuade him to sample hers at the very moment when he could blemish her reputation.

By thunder! He had fled from Fortenbury Park to avoid the parson's mouse-trap, which was baited with the promise of sweet kisses. Now, here he was at Dunsworthy Dower Cottage with his mind so focused on his desire to kiss Miss Rosie that even the theft of his horse and Wandersee's seemed insignificant.

He needed to get away from the cottage and temptation or he would start thinking about quickly following his brother down the aisle. Marriage was most definitely not in his plans for many years. He intended to go to Egypt and see the ancient writings for himself. He had to find a place to obtain another horse and leave Dunsworthy Dower Cottage.

Fast!

Aunt Millicent frowned at Rosie for what must have been the fifth time that day. Each time, Rosie swiftly scurried out of her aunt's way, not wanting to be chided again for being unthinking.

Rosie wanted to protest that she was not being thoughtless. She had far too many thoughts in her head. Not only about the horses stolen right out of their barn. Not only how Constable Powers had kissed her, and how she was so uncertain what to say to him after that kiss that she had hidden in the cottage while he came to examine the stable in hopes of finding some clue to identify the thieves. Not only thoughts of the conversation she had shared with Lord Fortenbury and Aunt Millicent last night. She had all those thoughts and more. Most centered on the wordless exchange between her and the viscount by the front door. No matter how many times she scolded herself—far more firmly than her aunt had—she could not get out of her mind the image of his face lowering toward hers.

Had she truly expected him to kiss her as boldly as Constable Powers had? Lord Fortenbury was a gentleman, as he had proved time and again during his short visit. Yes, she was the daughter of a baron, but she recognized the difference in their places. He held his family's title; she was the younger sister of the late baron, and their cousin now possessed both the title and the estate. Even if there had been no gap between them, she had been raised to know the canons of Society, and a young woman did not welcome the brazen buss of a man who was little more than a stranger.

But if that were true, why had she not been able to forget how she had hoped he would kiss her? Constable Powers had kissed her last night, so she knew what it was to be kissed by a man. Or did she? In her sister's stories, the heroine always was overwhelmed by the hero's kiss, but Rosie had not found the constable's kiss exceedingly pleasant. Nor had she thought it was horrible. It simply had kindled no more feeling than when her brother had given her a kiss on the cheek.

None of this made sense, but mayhap she could sort out her thoughts after Lord Fortenbury took his leave this afternoon. She must have her thoughts more under control before she arrived at his house for the wedding.

As for the constable, he had acted as if nothing extraordinary had happened except for the horses being stolen. She would be wise to emulate him. After all, Lord Fortenbury was leaving in a few minutes after having borrowed a horse from Dunsworthy Hall. As soon as the viscount was gone, everything would go back to the way it had been. Or so she hoped.

Tucking in a cloth over the basket she had packed with food for Lord Fortenbury on the first day of his journey back to Bath, for he now intended to go directly home, she picked it up. She carried the borrowed books under her other arm. She was able to smile at her aunt as they went out to see the viscount on his way. Her spirits rose as the rain-freshened air invited her to take a deep breath. This was her favorite time of the year, when the hectic whirl of harvesting the kitchen garden and putting up the food for winter was over and winter had not yet come to imprison them in the cottage.

The sun was brilliantly bright, enjoying its reflection in the rapidly shrinking puddles. Birds called from the trees and from atop the barn. Her aunt's beloved chrysanthemums were proudly displaying their deep colors around the edge of the wall.

Lord Fortenbury turned from where he had been talking with Moss and smiled. Rosie wondered how that expression could seem even more scintillating than the sunshine. He looked dashing in his riding coat and buckskin breeches. He had put the polish back onto his boots, for they were no longer dull with dust. No sign of the scholar remained, and, as he rested one arm on the saddle of his borrowed horse, he could have been a prime rake ready to break young women's hearts. She looked down at the basket before her own visage divulged her unsteady thoughts.

"Miss Dunsworthy," he said, "you always anticipate what your guest is thinking."

"We hope you will enjoy the light nuncheon we prepared for you." Aunt Millicent's voice now had warmed from the icy edge it had had last night. Although her aunt had said nothing, Rosie knew Aunt Millicent was despairing about a crime happening to a guest at Dunsworthy Dower Cottage.

Her aunt nudged her with an elbow, and Rosie held out the basket.

"Can I hope that this contains another piece of your strawberry tart, Miss Rosie?" he asked.

"We finished that last night, but there are some of the blackberry muffins we had for breakfast," she replied, relieved that she could. She had been afraid the words would not come this afternoon.

"'Tis a good thing that my visit here was brief." He patted his stomach. "I would be as broad as yon carriage if I remained here and continued to partake of your excellent cooking. I cannot guess how you and Miss Dunsworthy retain your charmingly slender shapes."

Aunt Millicent chuckled, and Rosie wondered if the viscount had been forgiven for everything. "There is always more than enough to do about here to keep one working off anything one eats."

"Then I should be on my way before you find some task for me to tend to." He bowed over her hand as he had when he arrived. "Once again, Miss Dunsworthy, I do thank you for your hospitality."

"I am so sorry that—"

He held up a single finger. "Do not feel the need to apologize for what is not your fault. Constable Powers assures me he will do all he can to find the stolen horses. As you should realize but I wish to assure you again, nothing that has happened lessens my gratitude to you for your kindness in opening your door to me." He gave them a wry grin. "I do have to be honest and own that I wish that the pad-thieves had not been so willing to open a door as well."

"I apologize again."

"No, I should apologize. I did not mean for my teasing to distress you more."

"It has not." She glanced at Rosie, then went to where Moss was now working to clean the interior of the carriage. From where she stood, Aunt Millicent would have a clear view of both Rosie and the viscount.

Rosie drew out the books and handed them to him. "Thank you, my lord, for sharing these and your opinions on them with me."

"Did I share my opinions?"

"A few."

"I have more than a few, but we shall have to indulge airing those opinions later."

"Yes." She was sure he could hear her heart pounding with excitement at the thought of another quiet conversation. A conversation that could lead to . . . She quelled that thought before it could tempt her further.

"You may wish to try these books, Rosie." He pulled two thick volumes out of the sack behind his saddle. As he stored the books she had read and hooked the basket onto his saddle, he added, "They are ones that I purchased on my most recent trip to London. Fortunately I brought the bag into the cottage with me, so they were not taken as well."

"But if they are valuable—"

"They will be safer with you and in Wandersee's carriage than on the horse."

She could not argue with him. Thieves were only one problem that faced a rider. Filth from the road could easily damage a book. She turned the books to read the titles on the spine and smiled. "This author wrote one of the other books you lent me."

"You expressed interest in his writing when we discussed his work at Jordan Court, so I thought you should read it as well. You can tell *me* if it is as informative as his previous work."

"You haven't read it yet?"

He shook his head. "Henry has given me very little time to read uninterrupted. He seems to find endless questions to pose to me as if he considers me an expert on the issue of weddings. Please read it. *You* will not be intruded upon during the next week."

"Thank you." She did not want to tell him that thoughts of his unexpected call would pester her along with the anticipation of seeing him once more. He had been here such a short time, but so much had happened to change her during a single day.

"I look forward to you enlightening me."

"About the information in these books? I collect that you know more already than I could ever learn from these books."

"You can enlighten me about what awaits within these covers." His eyes twinkled. "Or mayhap you can enlighten me about weddings, so I can share that information with my brother."

"I have had little experience with weddings, other than my sister's."

"Mayhap Henry will heed your words of wisdom, even so. My only other recourse is to keep him foxed until the wedding, so he goes about with a simple smile on his face. I do hope you will have a chance to read at least one of these books before we next speak, so our conversation can be on something other than the ceremony and the wedding breakfast."

Rosie laughed at his dreary tone. "I will have the luxury of much time to read on our journey to Fortenbury Park."

"So you do not suffer from carriage-sickness?"

She shook her head. "Fortunately, no, as long as I ride facing forward, and, to own the truth, I reread part of Professor MacDonald's other book after our conversation, so I shall be eager to see what else he has to say."

"You reread it last night?"

"This morning."

"Odd, I thought I heard someone up and about in the house last night."

"Barley likes to wander about at night." Rosie was glad that she could reply with the truth so her cheeks would not flame. She did not want him to guess how scarce sleep had been for her last night. "I hope he did not keep you awake too much."

"Not at all." He smiled. "Your dog has very furtive footfalls."

"It comes from sneaking up on rabbits. It is too bad that he had no interest in protecting the stable as he does the house. Otherwise the horses might not have been taken."

"He is a very good-natured dog."

"True. If he had been outside, he most likely would have escorted the thieves to the stable and stood guard so nobody disturbed *them* while they snuck away with the horses."

He laughed.

"Have a good journey, my lord," she said.

"I shall not say farewell, but *à bientôt*." He took her hand as he had Aunt Millicent's, but he did not bow politely over it. Instead he drew her toward the low wall between the house and the road. They were, she noted, still within her aunt's view, but far enough away so their voices would not reach Aunt Millicent's ears.

He sat her on it, then sat beside her. With his hand balanced on a stone behind her, she would have needed only to edge toward him a spare inch to lean her head on his shoulder. His shoulder appeared broad enough to offer her a generous cushion.

She did not move, aware that her aunt and Moss were close by. Also she could not help recalling how Constable Powers had kissed her only a short distance away. She started to edge forward to stand, then realized if she did, he might ask questions she would not want to answer. It was better to remain on the wall until she had an excuse to get up that he would not question.

"I look forward," she said, "to seeing the pieces of Egyptian tablets that you keep at Fortenbury Park. To own the truth, I look forward to seeing them even more after reading the books you lent me. I almost feel as if I can decipher some of the symbols."

"I would be glad to show you how complicated a tablet truly is. I have come to recognize many of the symbols, but the meaning continues to elude me. However, I would be glad to teach what little I have learned."

"Really?" She shifted so she faced him. "I would be so grateful to learn what you can teach me, my lord."

"Rupert."

"Excuse me?"

"I would prefer that you call me Rupert. If we are going to study together, I believe it would offer more camaraderie to our circumstances."

She smiled. "I agree as long as you agree to call me Rosie."

"I like calling you Miss Rosie."

"You do?" she asked, startled. Unlike Constable Powers, who was so predictable, she never could guess what Lord—Rupert—might say next.

"Actually, I like calling you Miss Primrose even more."

She wagged her finger at him in an imitation of her aunt. "You know I don't like that name."

"You don't?" He caught her finger in his hand, closing his own fingers around it. "Finally something we disagree about."

Staring at his hand that held her finger, she dampened her abruptly arid lips. She should say something. What? Her thoughts were scrambled as his flesh warmed her skin.

"I suspect there may be other things we disagree on," she replied, slipping her finger from within his. She stood, wanting to put some distance between them before she did something more out of hand. Something like reaching for his fingers again.

"I hope so." He set himself on his feet and reached for the horse's reins, which were looped around the dash of the carriage. "It is always much more interesting when studying together to have diverse opinions. That requires one to justify one's own thoughts."

"I look forward to seeing the fragments next week, Rupert."

His smile became even warmer when she spoke his name. "I shall see you within the week then." He chuckled. "That is, unless I find myself in need of a quiet sanctuary again."

"I trust you can endure the hullabaloo for the few remaining days until the wedding," she said as her aunt gave her a look that suggested their conversation had gone on long enough and that Rosie should not delay the viscount further from setting upon his way.

"With your faith in me, I shall do my best to live up to your expectations." Rupert's smile included her aunt, too, and Rosie found it far simpler to breathe again.

Aunt Millicent laughed as she came closer and shook her head. "I believe you are hoaxing us."

"Mayhap so. Mayhap not." He swung up into the saddle with an ease that bespoke of the hours he must be accustomed to riding. "I bid you *à bientôt*, Miss Dunsworthy, until you arrive at Fortenbury Park. Enjoy your reading, Rosie."

"Yes, I will, thank you," she replied, not having to look at her aunt to know that Aunt Millicent was regarding both her and Rupert with surprise.

He waved to Moss and steered his horse slowly out of the stableyard. When he reached the road, he set the horse to a faster speed.

"Well," Aunt Millicent said, smiling.

"Yes, well." Rosie gave her aunt a smile back. It was useless to pretend she was not anticipating their visit to Fortenbury Park even more than before Rupert's call. Seeing the stone tablets—and Rupert—was going to be so exciting! She would concentrate on that and not how she would be surrounded by the family's other guests.

Her smile broadened. There was no reason for anyone to pay attention to Rosie Dunsworthy. She would spend all her time reading and studying and examining the hieroglyphs on the stones.

Turning back to the cottage, she began to sing a cheery song that was flooding her head with its notes. It was the same melody that had come into her mind on the village green, and she knew she must come up with some words to go with the music.

She wondered what rhymed with Rupert.

# CHAPTER SIX

When she woke, it took Rosie a few seconds to remember why she shivered with such excitement. Her heart beat with the rhythm of a cloudburst upon a carriage roof. Her lips refused to turn any way but up. An unquenchable desire to giggle filled her, and she wanted to dance with the delight of a child discovering that Twelfth Night and all its revels had finally arrived. With a laugh as liquid as the sunlight flowing through the window, she submerged the yearning, for Aunt Millicent would deem her mad.

But how could she not be excited? Here she was in an inn less than a day's ride from Bath and Fortenbury Park. The days since Rupert rode away on his borrowed horse had been busy ones.

Constable Powers had called several times, but each visit had been aimed at giving them an update on the search for the stolen horses. On the most recent, just before they left for Bath, the constable had brought the good news that a horse matching the description of Rupert's Osiris was going to be sold at an upcoming market day. Mayhap the thieves were about to show their hand because they believed Rupert had left the parish and would not return.

Not once had Constable Powers given her more than a passing glance. Was he ashamed of his cocksure actions, or had he been as unmoved by the kiss as she had? She could not know without asking, and she had no intention of doing that.

She was on her way to Fortenbury Park for a wedding, so she should be thinking of that and the song that was swirling through her head. The melody was complete, but not the words. She thought about them each time she had a chance. So far she had two lines:

*The seasons turn, and color is born once more on the trees;*
*All too soon it will be gone, leaving nothing more than memories.*

She was not satisfied with the two lines, but she would revise them once she had the rest of the song's lyrics done. If only she could devise the next two lines of the song, but they had been eluding her. Creating such songs was a secret pleasure she had not shared with anyone, even though both Aunt Millicent and Bianca were always teasing her about singing all through the day. She suspected Aunt Millicent would be aghast to discover her niece was interested in writing music for more than her own pleasure. Such pursuits would bring ruin to the Dunsworthy name, because, while great opera librettists were acclaimed, only the lowest levels of society created music appropriate for the common voices that filled a theater.

Rosie slid out of the bed she had shared with Aunt Millicent. Her aunt was already gone, but Rosie knew Aunt Millicent would go no farther than the common room without her. The inn was not elegant, but the supper had been good. She hoped breakfast was the same. As she dressed in a light green gown, she caught her reflection in the glass. Her hair was down around her shoulders, and she could be mistaken for someone far younger than she was.

With a grimace, she twisted her hair up in a proper coiffure. She started to pin it in place, then let it fall about her shoulders. She had been ignoring her trepidation, trying to tell herself it was all anticipation, but she could not bamblusterate herself any longer. It was not finding the next lines of her song that bothered her. She was unsure how she would handle being in the crowds at Fortenbury Park.

When she met Rupert at Jordan Court, she had found his conversation about ancient Egypt fascinating and she had been able to ask him questions about his studies. It had been almost as easy to speak with Rupert when he was calling at Dunsworthy Dower Cottage. She had hoped words would come just as readily at his estate. Mayhap they would with him. However, she could not fool herself into believing that talking with his guests would be simple. She always found it impossible to give voice to even the simplest commonplaces when there was a crowd about. It was not that she never could think of things to say. That part was effortless. What was hard was forcing those words past her lips.

Since Rupert had left Dunsworthy Dower Cottage, Aunt Millicent had tried to encourage her to say more at the gatherings that would be held in anticipation of Mr. Jordan's wedding day. Aunt Millicent had told her over and over that no one would laugh or think what she had said was inappropriate. That might have helped if those were the things Rosie dreaded, but that advice had been more appropriate for her sister. Still, Bianca never was tongue-tied. Rosie was not certain what she was afraid might happen, and that very not knowing kept her silent.

Readying her hair for the day's journey and their arrival at Fortenbury Park, Rosie stuffed her night-clothes and hairbrush into her bag. She hurried down the stairs, glad to see Aunt Millicent waiting with some sweet buns. That meant the carriage was set to leave, and Rosie would be able to eat her breakfast while reading the final chapters of the book by Professor MacDonald.

The book was fascinating, just as Rupert had suggested it would be. Some of the theories proposed were based on ideas Rosie had never heard of. She wondered if Rupert had and hoped he would clarify the information for her.

She had only a little bit of the book left, and she would finish it on the way to Fortenbury Park. Losing herself in the pages would keep her from having to think about anything but seeing Rupert and his Egyptian fragments. *That* she looked forward to.

With a contented sigh, Rosie turned the last page and closed the book. It had been intriguing from the first page to the final one. So many ideas whirled through her head, and she wanted to explore each one further. She wondered what other books Rupert might have at his country house.

But Aunt Millicent would not be pleased if Rosie shut herself away and read during the visit. Her aunt had warned her about that when they were getting into the carriage this morning.

"I know you are enthralled by what you are reading," Aunt Millicent had said while Moss checked the carriage as he did each time they stopped.

"It is unbelievable! So much information is awaiting whoever can decipher the strange symbols." She again had to keep her feet from twirling her about in an excited dance. "Imagine if we were able to. It would—"

"We?"

"Rupert and I." She had smiled as she stepped up into the carriage. "The books he has lent me have opened my imagination to all sorts of possibilities. When I read the others he has—"

Again Aunt Millicent had interrupted her, something she did only when unsettled. "Rosie, you must recall the reason why we have been invited to Fortenbury Park."

"I remember." Her excitement had drained away as she looked at her aunt's somber expression.

"You will be expected to participate in the events leading up to the wedding. You must not huddle in your room with a book."

"I know."

Her disappointment must have come through in those words, because her aunt had reassured her that Rupert might allow her to borrow more of his books to read when they returned to the cottage.

Rosie glanced across the carriage to see that her aunt was now dozing. Aunt Millicent always found traveling very relaxing. Rosie wished she could be that nonchalant about the events ahead of them. The only weddings she had attended were ones in the village church. She doubted if anything about the wedding of Henry Jordan and Jenna Wallace would be so simple. It would be as grand as Mr. Jordan's incredible house near Plymouth.

Holding the book to her bodice, she thought of the confection of a dress that Aunt Millicent had remade for her from one worn during her aunt's shortened Season. The dress had been hopelessly out of style, reflecting what had been worn more than a decade ago. Now the gown, the color of creamy butter, was glorious and resembled the gowns they had seen in fashion-plates sent from London. It would be perfect for the ball the evening before the wedding.

The carriage slowed and bounced. Aunt Millicent opened her eyes, and Rosie peeked out the window to see that they were passing between two stone pillars. Trees edged the side of the road, and the grass beneath them was as perfect as a painting. They must have reached Fortenbury Park.

But where was the house? She started to stretch her head out the window to look, but Aunt Millicent chided, "Do not poke from the window like a pup sniffing the air."

"There is so much to see." She let the excitement consume her trepidation again.

Aunt Millicent chuckled. "You will have a chance, I am certain, to explore much of Fortenbury Park and mayhap even Bath while we are here. You need not try to see all of it at once."

Rosie kept her elbow on the bottom of the window but turned to her aunt. "This is so exciting. I have heard about Bath all my life and how the *haut monde* comes here to sample the waters. I wonder if they are as noxious as I have heard."

"Mayhap you will have the chance to discover the answer yourself. But do not expect too much,

Rosie. The *ton* does not spend as much time here now as they do in London."

"But we are here in Bath, so you will have a chance to be among the *ton* again. Mayhap this time will make up for some of what you missed."

Aunt Millicent chuckled. "Despite what you and your sister seem to think, I do not regret putting an end to my only Season. I was quite homesick for Dunstanbury, if you must know the truth."

"I thought you were glad to come home because of that gentleman you fell in love with and it did not work out and you wished to put it and the man named Quinn far behind you and . . ." Rosie clamped her lips closed. Why was *she*, of all people, babbling like a gabbler?

"You thought wrong." Aunt Millicent's smile became stiff. "How many times have I warned you that you need to avoid listening to gossip? It is bad enough in Dunstanbury where everyone seems eager to know everyone else's bread-and-butter. Among the Polite World, it can quickly lead you astray, for some of what you hear may be aimed at tarnishing someone's reputation."

Rosie nodded, chastised. Yet, she was also curious. Once, before they went to Jordan Court and the weekend where Rosie was introduced to Rupert, she and Bianca had asked their aunt if she had ever been in love. Aunt Millicent had mentioned a suitor called Quinn, saying nothing else about him. Her face, when she spoke his name, had been rigid. Rosie could not recall ever seeing that expression on her aunt's face either before or since . . . until now.

The expression made Rosie want to weep. If Aunt Millicent was working so hard to hide her feelings about that man, they must still be fragile. Yet so many years had passed. Had her aunt been mourning that lost love all those years?

To hide the tears that must be bright in her eyes, Rosie looked out the window at the passing trees. Mayhap Rupert could offer some insight into this. He was a part of the *ton*. Any information he might have could be the very thing to mend Aunt Millicent's heart, which remained broken so many years later.

"Fortenbury Park is beyond anything that *I* have seen." Aunt Millicent was wearing her customary warm smile again as she changed the subject. "I am surprised that Lord Fortenbury could not find a haven within such a house to escape his brother's intrusions."

"Mayhap Mr. Jordan is very persistent."

"I would say rather that the reason the viscount gave us for his call was not altogether the truth."

Rosie was about to jump to Rupert's defense, stating that he was an honest man, but she halted herself. She knew very little about him, other than his interest in the ancient Egyptian writing. Certainly she never would have guessed before she sat beside him on the settee that he had any thoughts of kissing her. Nor had she given any consideration to what she would do if he did. Now she could think of little else.

"What possible reason could he have had?" she asked, glad for the conversation that required her to focus on what her aunt said. That pushed aside those thoughts of Rupert's face so close to hers.

"Speculating about that will be futile, for he is the only one who knows that. If you are curious, you might ask him."

"I doubt that would be worthwhile. He avoided answering me before when I asked."

Aunt Millicent gave Rosie a curious look but said nothing as the carriage slowed in front of a massive house. It must contain scores of rooms behind its weathered stone walls. Chimneys sprouted in a mad parade across the roof, and windows sparkled back the sunlight.

How had she not seen any of it before? It was at least twice the size of the grand house in Plymouth. Even Dunsworthy Hall would be overwhelmed by the house. When she saw crenellations along a wall curving away from the road, she wondered how many years the oldest sections of the house had stood. It looked as if it had been raised shortly after the Conquest.

As the carriage stopped, the door opened. Rosie realized that someone had been watching for the carriage's arrival. A man emerged dressed in a pleasant blue livery. In fact, it was very nearly the shade of Aunt Millicent's eyes.

The carriage door was opened, and they were handed out. Rosie discovered they stood on a brick area that looked as weathered as the house. Mayhap it had been part of the gate to the original house. Then anyone arriving might not have been as warmly welcomed.

Moss jumped down from the box and showed the man who had opened the carriage door where the luggage was stored. Two other men in the same livery hurried to join them.

When her gaze followed them, Moss's gaze caught her eye. He gave her a lazy wink, and she smiled.

"Rosie," murmured her aunt.

Again chastened but glad for Moss's teasing,

which indicated he was enjoying the show of ostentation as much as she was, she saw her aunt waiting with another man in blue livery. He walked toward the door, and she hurried with her aunt to go into the house. She swallowed her gasp of astonishment when they stepped into the massive foyer.

The ceiling was several stories overhead, and both sides were edged by galleries that seemed to float in gilded splendor above their heads. She counted three levels of galleries overhead. Farther above, a huge brass chandelier with crystal decoration dropped from the center of a stained glass dome in the very center of the ceiling. Colored patterns of flowers and nymphs were distorted to a blur by the time they reached the black and white tiles of the foyer.

The liveried man did not give her a chance to look at the paintings on the wall or the finely made furniture edging the curved stairs leading up to the lowest gallery. He walked up the stairs without looking back. He must assume they would follow, and they did.

Rosie could not keep from thinking about the simple furniture and rooms at Dunsworthy Dower Cottage. How kind of Rupert to assure them that he felt quite at home in such comparatively simple surroundings when he was accustomed to the magnificence of Fortenbury Park!

As they reached the top of the steps, Mr. Jordan hurried toward them. He bowed over Aunt Millicent's hand, then Rosie's.

She smiled at him, seeing the resemblance between him and his older brother. Both had the same dark hair, although Mr. Jordan's was not so curly. Tall and well built, Mr. Jordan in another time would have been a fearsome sight in his family's armor atop his destrier. His enemies would have fled before the sight of him on that warhorse.

Again she was tempted to laugh. In his elegant, well-tailored brown coat and light-colored breeches, he regarded them with the twinkling eyes of an eager host. He fit perfectly into this time and this house, not the past. She could not let her fanciful thoughts betray her into making some silly *faux pas.*

"Welcome to Fortenbury Park!" Mr. Jordan said with a broad grin. "I was passing a window and chanced to see Wandersee's carriage arrive, and I was determined to come and thank you personally for coming for the wedding."

"We are delighted to have been invited," Aunt Millicent replied.

"Rupert is about somewhere. I know he wanted to be here to greet you." Confusion marred his face as his mouth twisted. "I do believe he said something about returning your hospitality. No, I must have misunderstood him."

Rosie exchanged a smile with her aunt. Clearly Rupert had not told his brother how he had sought sanctuary for a night at Dunsworthy Dower Cottage.

"I am not sure where he is," Mr. Jordan continued. "Why don't I have you shown to your rooms, and then . . ." He paused at the sound of footsteps to his right. "Rupert! There you are! Come and see who has come to join us."

Rosie spun to look to her left. Having the chance to speak with Rupert again was the very thing she had been anticipating so eagerly the past week. She did not wait for him to step out of the shadows. Taking a step forward, she said, "Rupert, I cannot wait to share with you what Professor MacDonald had to say about . . ."

She bit her lip to halt her babbling at the same moment her aunt put a cautioning hand on Rosie's arm. She did not need Aunt Millicent's warning, for she had seen what her aunt had.

A woman was at Rupert's side, her hand possessively on his arm. She had hair so ebony that it glowed with blue fire when she stepped out into the light from a nearby window. Every curve of her face was perfect to match those along her body. Her gown accented her body, displaying just enough of her full breasts to make a man curious about what he could not see. A gold pendant hanging from a string of pearls dropped into that valley to suggest there was more treasure to be discovered. She moved with a sinuous grace that set her pure white gown to shimmering in the sunlight.

She was beautiful and polished and a man's fantasy come to life—everything that country bumpkin Rosie Dunsworthy could never aspire to be.

"Lord Fortenbury," Aunt Millicent said as if this encounter were exactly as she had expected, "how kind of you to come and greet us! Mr. Jordan has already given us a lovely welcome to your home."

"I was about to send someone for you," Mr. Jordan added, "because I knew you wanted to know when Wandersee's carriage arrived."

Rupert continued to walk toward them, and Rosie continued to stare. She knew she should not. She could not halt herself. She wished she could look away from how the pretty brunette now had both hands on Rupert's arm, a clear sign that the woman considered the viscount hers. Rosie's smile must appear brittle, for she was certain it would shatter and fall away at any moment.

"You clearly have made better time than I had expected you to," Rupert said, his tone heavier than it had been when he took his leave of Dunsworthy Dower Cottage.

"The roads were not mired, and Moss is an excellent coachee." Aunt Millicent jabbed Rosie with her elbow.

Rosie knew what that meant. Aunt Millicent wanted her to say something instead of standing as mute as the people in the portraits along the gallery. Speaking was impossible. If she opened her mouth, she was sure to blurt out something that would humiliate both her and Aunt Millicent more.

If that was possible.

"Allow me to introduce you to another of the guests who has come to Fortenbury Park for Henry's wedding." Rupert edged away from the brunette so she had to release his arm, something that did not please her, Rosie noted. "This is Ophelia King. Ophelia, I take great pleasure in introducing you to Miss Millicent Dunsworthy and her niece Primrose Dunsworthy."

"How nice to meet you!" Miss King smiled, and her expression was as warm as the sunshine flowing through the stained glass overhead. "I have met so many people since I arrived. You must grant me the privilege of introducing you about during the afternoon. And you must join me and some of my friends for tea." Her voice was a pleasing pitch, and it had a soft huskiness that suggested she was sharing her words only with each one she spoke to, making each feel special. "We do want to get to know you much better."

Rupert smiled coolly as Ophelia continued to prattle about the gatherings that she would make certain the Dunsworthy women were part of. She was acting as if she were the hostess of the wedding . . . and the house. He looked at Rosie, whose cheeks were the very shade of her namesake, and he guessed from that color and the way her hair was pushed back haphazardly beneath her bonnet that she had been eagerly looking out the carriage window during the last miles of the journey. That was no surprise, because she had an innate curiosity that matched his.

But she had not said a word after her initial greeting. He would have to be a widgeon not to understand why. He had seen her dismay when her gaze alighted on Ophelia's covetous hand. By thunder! He had thought that Rosie was different from other women who seemed eager to vie for his attention in the hopes of obtaining a title and becoming chatelaine of Fortenbury Park.

He must have misjudged Rosie, either before or now. Or had his own actions suggested to an impressible country lass that a kiss was the prelude to an offer of marriage? He had not even kissed her, despite his many thoughts of doing so. He must take care not to say something out of hand until he had a chance to determine which. If luck was on his side, he was mistaken now.

"I look forward," he said to Rosie when Ophelia paused to take a breath, "to discussing what you have read."

"Read?" Ophelia asked. "About what?"

He gave Rosie a chance to answer, then realized she would not. Mayhap she could not, for he knew how easy it was for her to be intimidated into silence by those she did not know well.

He said, "Rosie shares an interest in my studies of trying to understand the Egyptian written language."

Ophelia sniffed. "Really, Rupert, must you speak of such musty subjects now? From the way they look, these ladies must be greatly fatigued from their journey here, and they surely wish a chance to rid themselves of the dirt and fustiness of traveling."

Miss Dunsworthy put her hand up to the brim of her bonnet, but Rosie continued to wear that smile that did not look like her customary one. It was chilly and, if she had been any of the women he had met among the *ton*, he would have labeled it practiced. Yet, that seemed to contradict the honest, intelligent woman he had spoken with at her aunt's cottage.

Again he waited a minute for Rosie to say something, but she remained as unspeaking as Rupert became each time Henry asked about Rupert's plans to marry. His fingers curled into fists at that vagrant thought. Henry could not resist sticking his nose into everything Rupert tried to do. Had his brother suggested that Ophelia seek out Rupert a few minutes ago because he had seen the carriage coming up the avenue to the house's front door? Had Henry hoped that Rupert would be wise enough to see Ophelia's plentiful charms when compared side-by-side with artless Rosie?

Those were unworthy thoughts, and he shoved them aside as he sought something to say to put an end to the silence. It had become so thick at the top of the stairs he feared he was going to suffocate.

Rupert motioned to a footman and smiled at Miss Dunsworthy, who was regarding him and

Ophelia with a complete lack of expression. If he looked at Rosie, he was unsure whether he could maintain the pretense that everything was just as it should be.

"Arnold will take you to the rooms we have set aside for you," he said. "I believe you will enjoy them, for they offer a lovely view of the water garden."

"Thank you, my lord." Miss Dunsworthy poked Rosie with her elbow as Rupert had seen her do before.

Rosie's expression did not change as she said in a dutiful tone, "Yes, thank you so very much."

"When you are settled," Rupert said, "mayhap we can find some time to discuss your opinions of Professor MacDonald's work."

"Yes."

He hoped she would say more, but she simply nodded her thanks to his brother before walking toward the staircase to the upper floors. The footman led Rosie and Miss Dunsworthy up the stairs, and none of them looked back. Tearing his eyes from Rosie, he caught Ophelia's triumphant smile.

"What a sweet pair," Ophelia murmured.

"You will like them," Henry gushed. "Miss Dunsworthy is a true heroine. She gave up her own chance for marriage to take care of her orphaned nieces and nephew when she was in the midst of her first Season."

"That is a sacrifice few women would be willing to make." Her beguiling laugh trilled through the hallway as if she had made a joke. "Henry, you are looking particularly dashing today. Do come and tell me what has put that smile upon your face."

"I thought you would be sitting with Her Grace at this hour."

"On my way, so you can escort me there like the dear chap you are." She slipped her hand through his arm and flashed a coquettish smile back at Rupert.

Did she think he would fly into a jealous pelter because she was flirting with his brother? Mayhap she *wished* he would. He bowed his head toward her and said, "Let Her Grace know that I have spoken to the kitchen about having her tea mixed in exactly the manner she prefers."

"You are a dear, too." She brushed her lips against his cheek, letting them linger a heartbeat longer than etiquette allowed between friends. Wafting her full eyelashes at him, she smiled. "Don't forget that you are *my* escort into dinner tonight, dear Rupert."

"I would never forget such an honor," he replied automatically before she walked away with his brother.

Rupert leaned one hand on the marble railing that edged the top of the stairs. He glanced again toward where Rosie and her aunt had disappeared up the stairs. When he sensed eyes on him, he turned to see a footman standing nearby. The young man was trying not to smile, but his eyes twinkled merrily.

By thunder! There was nothing amusing about Ophelia's attempts to pursue him and Rosie's mental perturbation at witnessing Ophelia's flirting. He had hoped Ophelia would take his absence for disinterest, but she proved the adage that absence makes the heart grow fonder. He doubted her heart had anything to do with her actions, for Ophelia made no secret of the fact that she intended for there to be the announcement of another Jordan wedding before Henry's was celebrated.

When the door opened below, Rupert waved the

footman down the stairs. His brother's wedding was becoming even more complicated than it already had been, the very thing he had wanted to avoid.

Ophelia had clearly dismissed Rosie as no competition in her unending quest to catch Rupert's attention and persuade him to propose. Otherwise Ophelia would have found some excuse to probe more deeply into how Rupert knew these two women. He sighed under his breath.

He should have warned Rosie that things would not be as genial and jovial here as they had been at his brother's estate of Jordan Court near Plymouth. Ophelia was not the only woman who seemed to think it was her duty to save him from the rigors of ongoing bachelorhood. In retrospect, he realized what he should have known all along. Rosie's company was so pleasant because she spoke of matters that had nothing to do with matches and matrimony.

How had he missed such an obvious truth? He seldom overlooked such a fact. And now he had accused her—in his mind—of being like Ophelia. He owed Rosie an apology. And he would give it to her in person.

Soon.

# CHAPTER SEVEN

Miss King had a rare gift for making the smallest matter seem to have the greatest importance, Rosie decided as she listened to the brunette entertain the other ladies with her comments. Holding court would have been a better description, but Rosie did not want to be overly judgmental. Rosie pretended to listen to an inventory of Miss King's woes with her *couturière*. While Miss King rambled on and on, Rosie took the time to look around the circle of women who seemed to hang on every word she spoke.

Jenna Wallace, Henry Jordan's betrothed, sat on Miss King's left. Miss Wallace had made Rosie and her family welcome at Mr. Jordan's gathering in Plymouth last month, and she was doing the same now. Miss Wallace was so short that the top of her head did not reach her fiancé's shoulder. Soft brown curls edged her heart-shaped face and accented her eyes of the same color. Rosie thought she resembled one of the cherubs on the friezes around the ceiling of what was called the small parlor, even though the room was larger than the whole of Dunsworthy Dower Cottage.

Miss Wallace's mother had the chair next to her daughter, and Miss Wallace's two aunts sat on a white settee across from Rosie. Her mother and one aunt were of the same diminutive size, but one aunt was both tall and wide. Lines at the corners of their eyes hinted that they laughed often, but they had not had a chance to speak since Miss King began her lament about the lack of imagination on the part of her *modiste* in London.

A Jordan cousin whose first name Rosie could not recall, and an aunt who was Rupert's mother's sister, completed the circle. Aunt Millicent had demurred when offered the chance to sit in on the conversation, saying she wanted to tend to some matters in her room. Wishing that she had not let Miss King persuade her to join the ladies in the small parlor, Rosie resisted glancing at the longcase clock in the corner *again.*

"Don't you think so, Miss Dunsworthy?" Miss King asked, turning toward her.

Rosie blushed. She should have been heeding the conversation more closely. Every word she had ever spoken vanished from her mind along with any hint of what Miss King had been lamenting about.

Mrs. Wallace reached across the table between her and Rosie and patted Rosie's hand. "Ophelia, my dear," she said, her tone suggesting that she did not consider Ophelia King at all dear, "you are putting Miss Dunsworthy into an awkward situation by asking her about *modistes* in Town. I do believe that Miss Dunsworthy has mentioned at least once that she has not been to London recently, preferring the country while she has been in mourning for her brother, who died while defending our country against that Corsican demon."

Rosie raised her eyes to Mrs. Wallace's kind ones and smiled. Beside her mother, Miss Wallace was fighting not to grin and losing the battle. She wanted to thank both of them, but to do so would be an insult to Miss King.

"Ah, yes, I do recall that." Miss King launched into another monologue about the terrible taste of the water at the Pump Room in Bath.

Keeping her back stiff as she sat properly on her chair, Rosie tried to slow her breathing so that her color would return to normal. She doubted if it had, for her cheeks continued to burn, even when the others began to take their leave. She took advantage of that and excused herself as well. If Miss King heard her, the brunette gave no sign, for she did not falter in her comments about someone whose name Rosie did not recognize.

When Rosie emerged from the room onto one of the galleries, she released her breath in a relieved sigh. Until now, she had believed it was a far worse curse to fail to speak than to be a prattler. She was beginning to believe she had been completely wrong.

"Do not let her disconcert you," Miss Wallace said from where she had obviously been waiting for Rosie in the corridor. She stepped around a high candleholder made of painted ceramic. "Ophelia always likes to keep herself as the center of attention."

"I saw that." Rosie started to flush anew, then laughed as Miss Wallace did. "I appreciate your kindness and your mother's for rescuing me when I had no answer for Miss King's question."

"We knew Ophelia was trying to put you in an uneasy situation. She must have been aware that you were not prepared to answer her question when you have been remaining close to home."

Rosie smiled. "You are being kind. Even if I had been able to find the proper words with everyone listening, I must own that I had allowed my attention to wander. I must own, as well, that I had no interest in her litany of woes."

Miss Wallace laughed again. "It is good to see you again, Miss Dunsworthy. Your way of speaking plainly and only when you have something worthwhile to say is refreshing." She smiled. "May I address you as Rosie?"

"Of course."

"And you shall use my given name as well." Jenna took Rosie's hand and squeezed it with enthusiasm. "I am pleased that you and your aunt are here a few days before the wedding. It will give you and me time to become better acquainted."

"I look forward to that."

"Please set aside some time for us to speak together."

"Me?" Rosie laughed again. "*You* are the bride. Your time is full now."

Miss Wallace held up her empty hands. "You would be surprised how little I have to do when both my mother and Henry are double-checking every detail." She rolled her eyes. "Double-checking and double-checking again."

"So the wedding will be perfect."

"I hope so. To own the truth, I have been doing a bit of double-checking myself." Her eyes narrowed as she added, "And I understand your time is going to be occupied with studying those dusty old stones with Rupert."

"He told me that he would teach me more about the writing on them. It is a fascinating study."

"I am sure you two find it so. Do you know where these lessons will be?"

Rosie regarded Jenna with bafflement. "I assume they will be in his book-room where he keeps the tablets."

"His book-room?" Jenna tapped her chin. Lowering her voice, she leaned toward Rosie. "Take care and watch your back with Ophelia, Rosie. She does not intend to let anyone get in the way of her schemes to make sure Rupert becomes her husband."

"Rupert and I are studying the fragments together. That is all." Her voice cracked on the words, but she reminded herself that they were the truth. Since her arrival at Fortenbury Park yesterday, she had seen Rupert only twice. She had exchanged no more words during their second encounter—at dinner—than at their first by the staircase from the foyer.

"I hope Ophelia will believe that. If she gets it into her mind that you are competition, she will do everything she can to make your life miserable."

She nodded, again unsure what to say. She did not want to disparage Miss King by agreeing, but what Jenna was telling her was nothing she had not figured out herself. Miss King had made her place in Rupert's life clear yesterday when Rosie met her.

With another smile and invitation to join her for tea, Jenna rushed off to answer her mother's call of her name.

Rosie walked in the opposite direction, because she did not want to chance being drawn back into the monologue that still was going on in the parlor.

Her intention of returning to her room was dashed when she realized she was wandering from one unfamiliar corridor to another. All seemed to come to an end at a window that overlooked the gardens, but not one of the rooms opening off the corridors was the one she had been given for her use.

Knowing she would never find her room in such a haphazard manner and not yet ready to own that she was lost—how Miss King would laugh if she discovered Rosie could not find her way about in the house!—she decided to go down the closest flight of stairs, go out into the garden, and come around the house to the front. From the foyer, she would be able to retrace the steps she had taken when she and Aunt Millicent arrived.

A fresh breeze greeted her as she emerged from the house into what looked like a knot garden. The well-trained bushes were shaped into intricate patterns and edged with small white stones that crunched beneath her with each step. Other shrubs had been allowed to grow higher, but even they had been sculpted into shapes nature had not intended them to take. It was almost bizarre to see a cone-shaped bush next to one as round as a ball. The very perfection was bothersome.

Much like Miss King.

Rosie frowned at her own thought. Jenna had been generous when she warned Rosie about Miss King, and Rosie had been just as ungrudging of the brunette who had attempted to embarrass her. Miss King's apparently innocuous question had been worded in such a way that no one could believe it was anything but an intentional interest in Rosie's opinion.

She shook her head. She would not be drawn

into the absurd games played by some within the *ton*. Aunt Millicent had warned her over and over during both the journey to Plymouth last month and the one to Fortenbury Park that a young woman must guard every word and every reaction with the greatest care.

Running her fingertips along the closely clipped bushes, Rosie began to hum the melody that filled her head. She had written a few more lines of words to go with the song. As she walked out of the knot garden, she followed a stone wall that was as high as her shoulder. Her steps took on the rhythm of the song as she began to sing the melody that soared like a hawk on the autumn air.

> *The seasons turn, and color is born once more on the trees;*
> *All too soon it will be gone, leaving nothing more than memories.*
> *Memories of red and gold and sunlight and a bird's lingering song,*
> *Memories of a gentle wind from the sea to warm the heart through the winter long.*
> *My heart is cold without you, when you are far from me and home.*
> *I wonder why you have left me unkissed and without your arms around me and . . .*

"Don't stop."

She looked across the high wall to see Rupert matching her steps on its far side. Her face burned, and she wondered how she could even speak. Singing was impossible now.

"Such a pretty song," he said with a smile. "I don't

think I have heard it before. Is it from Dunstanbury?"

"Yes."

"An old song?"

She shook her head.

"A new one?" he asked as he reached a stile and climbed over it to stand beside her.

Instead of answering, she stared at him. Every other time she had seen him, he had been wearing the finest of fashion. Now he wore a green coat with elbows so worn that the fabric was shiny. There was a patch on the knees of his dark brown breeches, and something had left a muddy stain on the front of his gold waistcoat. Only his boots looked familiar, because they bore the deep shine he had given them before leaving the cottage. His hat was set at a jaunty angle, and he had a gun tilted over his right shoulder.

He glanced at the gun and lowered it to the ground. "I don't intend to shoot you, if the thought of that is causing the dismay on your face, Rosie."

"I did not think that."

"Good!" He smiled.

Her own lips tilted, and she let her shoulders ease from their stiff pose.

"So tell me about the song."

She continued along the wall a few steps, then realized he was not following. She turned to look back at him. Only then did she discover how far she was from the house. No wonder he had looked at her with astonishment. The wall did not curve back toward the front of the house but edged the curve of the hill leading off into the distance.

"It is just a song," she said, not willing to own to the complete truth just yet.

"You sing it beautifully."

"Thank you."

"You should sing more often."

Her smile returned. "I do. Aunt Millicent says I sing too much."

"But I did not hear you singing when I was at Dunsworthy Dower Cottage."

"I don't sing when others are around."

With a chuckle, he walked toward her, offering his arm. "Then I am glad I did not announce myself when I heard you singing. However, I stand by my assertion. You should sing more often."

She put her hand within his elbow. When he continued along the wall rather than returning to the house, she was amazed how much relief coursed through her. She needed some fresh air to clear her head. Being so close to Rupert brought forth sensations she did not want to examine. She simply wanted to enjoy the chance to stroll with him as if they were at the cottage and everything was simpler.

"Will you?" he asked.

"Will I what? Are you asking me to sing?" she blurted. Her barriers to him slipped as his gaze pierced them.

"Only if you wish to. I would like to hear the rest of the song."

She laughed, knowing that if she tried to hide the truth with convoluted words, she would be playing the games Aunt Millicent had warned her were so prevalent among the *beau monde.*

"There is no more of the song," she said.

"You are singing a song you have forgotten?" He gave her a puzzled look.

"I have not forgotten it. There simply is no more of the song yet."

His dark brows rose as he chuckled. "Now I understand. You are creating this sensual song. Do you mourn for a lost lover?"

"No! One can know of lost love without experiencing it."

"Is that so?" He laughed. "You are a woman of many secrets, Primrose Dunsworthy."

"Please don't call me 'Primrose.'"

"As you wish, *Rosie*."

"And I do not have many secrets," she said, stepping around a mound of dirt in the grass, which was getting thicker and higher. "I simply do not tell everyone that I like to put words with the songs that play through my mind."

"That sounds like keeping a secret to me."

"Not to me."

He laughed again.

"Are you planning to hunt something?" Rosie asked to turn the conversation from her music.

"Actually I was looking for you."

"With a gun?"

"I went shooting earlier with some of the guests, and I had no chance to put it away when your aunt came to me, distressed because there was no sign of you."

She hesitated, then said, "I became lost in your house."

"That is not difficult to do. It is far larger than Dunsworthy Hall."

"Dunsworthy Hall is my cousin's home now."

He held her chin between his thumb and finger. She stared into his eyes as he bent until they were level with hers. She was unsure of the emotions she could see there, and she was even more unsure of her own.

"I am so sorry," he said quietly.

"Don't be sorry for me. I don't need you or anyone else feeling sorry for me. I felt sorry for myself long enough after my brother died and we moved out of Dunsworthy Hall even though I prefer the cottage to that dark and damp manor house. Now I am grateful for any opportunity to live comfortably with my aunt in Dunsworthy Dower Cottage."

"Where you can create your music whenever you wish?"

She used every bit of willpower she possessed to edge away from Rupert. Her feet fought her, making each step as difficult as if she were wading through knee-deep snow. She knew she should look away, but her gaze was held by his. Breaking that connection between them might mean losing everything they had shared.

But what they had shared must be allowed to go no further.

"Yes, whenever I wish." Knowing her answer was curt because he abruptly released her, she sighed. Words came too easily with Rupert, and she needed to learn to curb those that were a problem. "Thank you for not laughing at my silliness."

He stopped, and she had to as well because he took her hand and put it back on his arm. "There is nothing silly about the confusing corridors of Fortenbury Park. Every time we have a gathering, we find ourselves going upon an expedition to locate a missing guest or two. And it is completely understandable when you have so much on your mind beyond your song." His smile vanished. "I understand you and Jenna had a conversation in the wake of the gathering in the small parlor."

"Yes, we did."

"I am sure whatever was said can be remedied."

"What are you talking about?"

"You and Jenna. I was told that you spoke a few words and then left without—"

"Without what?" she asked, shocked that even such a mundane conversation would be viewed as something that might be of concern to their host. "Jenna and I had a pleasant conversation where we spoke about her upcoming wedding. There was nothing more to it than that."

"I am glad to hear that. When I was told otherwise, I thought it best to check on the truth myself."

"I do not know who came to you with such a story, but I urge you not to heed that person again. I have no idea why anyone would wish to do Jenna damage in your eyes."

"Or you." His mouth tightened.

Rosie looked away before her face could betray her. His simple answer told her the truth. Someone had carried tales about her to Rupert in an effort to disparage her. She wondered why, but she doubted he knew. Even if he did, she guessed he was too much a gentleman to divulge it.

Searching for something to ease the tension, she asked, "Did you shoot anything on your expedition this morning?"

"I was not after game. I was trying out this new gun which Henry brought from Manton's in London." He motioned for her to stand closer to the wall.

As she climbed to sit on the steps of another stile, Rupert sighted the gun on a tree near another section of the stone wall. She held her breath as his finger slowly contracted on the trigger. The gunpowder detonated with a crash that sent the birds spiraling skyward. Bark exploded to mark the site of the impact.

Rosie clapped her hands as he lowered the weapon.

"Thank you," he said with a half bow.

Sitting beside her, he reloaded the gun. He looked up as he pushed the top back on his powder horn and smiled.

"What is funny?" she asked.

"I was thinking what a hieroglyph would look like for a man with a gun rather than a spear."

She laughed. "What a silly thought!"

Standing, he held out his hand to her. She put hers on his palm and let him bring her to her feet. As she was about to thank him, he leaned the gun against the wall and grasped her arms. Slowly his hands slid down her arms until his fingers could weave through hers.

He whispered her name, and she raised her eyes from his hands to meet his gaze. She wanted to ask him what he wanted, but she knew. It was what she wanted, too. She tried to imagine his lips against hers, but could not. All she had for reference was Constable Powers's kiss, and she did not want to think that Rupert's would be the same.

Then he released her hands and picked up his gun. Staring at his back, she was curious why, unlike before, he had been the first to lower his eyes.

When he spoke, she sensed the false lightness in his voice. "I understand you want to go to Bath."

"Yes."

"Some of the guests are planning a sojourn in Bath, and I wondered if you would like to join us."

Rupert waited for Rosie's answer. He could not fault her for looking confused. One moment he was touching her; the next he was turning away. He talked to her about the ancient Egyptian writing, treating her as an equal; then he was murmuring her name with the desperation of a starving man.

By the time they reached the house, he was not sure what he had said on the way back. He had talked and talked and talked, leery of the quiet that would allow his thoughts to wander again to how luscious she felt beneath his fingers. No other woman had ever threatened to complicate his life as she did. Ophelia openly flirted with him, but he had learned to deflect her attempts to persuade him to compromise her. Rosie was the opposite, speaking with sincerity and trying to hide the passion that hid within her. He had sensed that passion when he discovered her genuine interest in his obsession with hieroglyphics, but he was learning with each meeting how many depths she possessed. Her music was an amazing opportunity to see beyond her quiet exterior.

When he saw several of the guests standing by carriages at the front of the house, he steered Rosie toward a side door. There was enough gossip about the Dunsworthy women already, as there was with anyone new to the closed circle of friends. He did not need to add to *on-dits* by openly displaying that he and Rosie had been walking alone beyond the gardens.

He closed the door behind them, shutting off the sound of conversations near the carriages. Rosie continued along the dusky corridor that led between the kitchen and the main section of the house. Setting his gun by the door, he caught her by the arm again.

"You did not answer my question," he said quietly

enough so no one but Rosie would be privy to his words. "Would you like to come to Bath with us?"

"I must ask Aunt Millicent." Her cheeks turned red, and he wondered what he had said to upset her. Or was it from the heat that burst through him whenever he touched her? She must be even more ill-prepared to deal with the powerful sensation than he was.

"And if she says yes, will you go? Or could it be that you have something else to hide from me?"

"I will go if she says yes."

"Good. Then I shall be glad to drive both of you into the city."

"You do not need to do that." She did not look up, but her ruddy hair was still lost against the furious shade on her cheeks. "I know you must be very busy with the wedding such a short time away."

"Don't you remember how I have already shown my desire to escape?"

A smile tilted her lips, and she finally raised her face. "So you will bolt only as far as Bath this time?"

"I would gladly go farther. Much farther." He chuckled. "However, Bath is as far as I have time to go today, and amid the twisting streets, it is unlikely that Henry will find me."

"Oh!" She put her fingers to her lips. "I promised Jenna that I would have tea with her and her mother this afternoon."

"We will be back long before then." He held out his hand. "Do you wish to go?"

She nodded. "Yes, I truly do."

"We need to find the others."

"Yes, we should do that." He did not move as he treated himself to a long, slow perusal of her from head to foot. With her high color and her hair plucked from its sedate style by the breeze, she was beguiling. But there was so much more to her than her outer beauty, and the enigma of an innocent who created such heartfelt music was a puzzle he wished to solve as much as he wanted to discover the key to the hieroglyphics.

Silencing the bewitching thoughts, he murmured, "You may go on bamboozling everyone else, but you shall not fool me any longer."

"What are you talking about?"

Taking her other hand, he said, "There is a rare passion in music that hints at the poignancy deep within you. You hide behind bashful ways, but I am beginning to suspect that flash of fire on your face has more to do with emotion than embarrassment."

"I assure you that I am exactly as I appear. It is just that I love music."

"You may believe what you are saying is true, but I think I am going to have to prove you wrong before you leave Fortenbury Park."

"You will be wasting your time, because I assure you that you are mistaken."

"It is my time, and I assure you that I am not." He smiled and watched her mouth grow round with astonishment as he added, "And I am going to have a grand time proving that to you."

# CHAPTER EIGHT

Aunt Millicent was thrilled to accept Rupert's invitation to join him and Rosie to ride in his elegant open carriage to Bath. So was Rosie, for she had shaken off her dismay at how he seemed to see aspects of her that she could not see herself. Letting her mind abide on his insight and how naked it made her feel was something she did not want to do when she was riding toward the Pulteney Bridge.

She listened to Rupert and Aunt Millicent chatting, but their voices were drowned out by the repetition of the song in her mind. Clasping her fingers in her lap was the only way to keep them from swaying with the rhythm of the notes lilting through her head. Why was the melody loudest whenever Rupert was around? Mayhap it was as simple as the song was a happy one, and being with Rupert, even when he was vexing her, made her happy.

Just before they drove onto the bridge, she could see below them the River Avon rushing on its way. Ducks gamely tried to swim against its current but managed only not to get swept downstream. Children lingered by the shore, watching the ducks and tossing out fishing lines. She saw nothing more before the buildings on the bridge blocked her view.

She leaned back on the bright blue seat and ran her fingers over the carriage's smooth white side. When her aunt patted her knee, Rosie smiled. She could sense Aunt Millicent's excitement in that brief touch. Before she had assumed the care of the Dunsworthy children, had Aunt Millicent come to Bath to enjoy the Polite World? Rosie wanted to ask and wondered why she had not already.

Rupert must have noted Aunt Millicent's eagerness as well because he asked, "Do you have anyone you would like to call upon while we are in the city, Millicent?"

Rosie smiled, glad that her aunt and Rupert had set aside the formality between them.

Aunt Millicent shook her head. "It has been so long since I last visited Bath that I believe I shall just enjoy looking upon it as if my eyes were beholding it for the first time."

"Excellent!" he replied. "It is fun to share an old sight with new eyes. I trust you will share what you see with me."

"Of course," Aunt Millicent replied.

"And you, Rosie? Will you share your opinions with me, too?"

Rosie nodded as his gaze caught hers as it had by the wall. Tempted to say that she found something new each time she looked into *his* eyes, she let Aunt Millicent interrupt that dangerous thought to point out the abbey with its soaring tower and the flying buttresses that reached up to the unbelievably tall windows. She followed Aunt Millicent's finger and listened while her aunt talked about the interior of the abbey.

With a laugh, Rupert said, "You speak with the sagacity of a native, Millicent. Have you been inside the abbey often?"

"Only once, but it was so beautiful that I have never forgotten it." She put her hand on Rosie's arm and smiled warmly as she did whenever she wandered through her memories of the times before tragedy first visited their family. "I was not much more than a child, and I believed that I had reached heaven just by walking through the door. Where else could one see such lifelike statues bathed in colored light from the windows?"

"Aunt Millicent is fond of sculpture," Rosie said.

"As fond as you are of music? Does she have a skill with sculpture as you do with writing songs?"

Before she could reply, Aunt Millicent asked, "Writing songs?"

"Surely," Rupert said with a smile, "you are familiar with Rosie's love of music."

"Yes. She is constantly humming one tune or another." Aunt Millicent's mouth became a perfect circle before she asked, "Are some of those songs of your own creation, Rosie?"

"A few."

"I had no idea."

Rupert chuckled. "She is in the midst of composing a song now. I heard her singing a few lines of it, but she tells me I must wait to hear the rest."

"I would like to hear it sometime." Aunt Millicent glanced at Rosie quickly, but Rosie did not understand what her aunt hoped to convey.

"As soon," Rosie said, "as it is finished. I had not planned to share it with anyone until then."

"So you intended to share it eventually?" asked Rupert.

She kept her smile in place with the greatest effort. "Eventually."

"Eventually can be a very long time from now."

"Yes."

When he laughed, Aunt Millicent did, too, but again she gave Rosie a glance that suggested her expression was meant to impart some information. Again Rosie had no idea what.

As her aunt deftly changed the subject to a mutual acquaintance who lived in a house just beyond Pulteney Bridge, Rosie relaxed against the cushions of the beautiful carriage. She must not make every look mean more than it did. Aunt Millicent might have meant nothing more than trying to keep Rosie in the discussion.

Looking around again, Rosie discovered that the city was much grander than Dunstanbury. It was more elegant than Plymouth, and she could almost believe the whole of Bath was a work of art created simply to be admired. The sunlight on the soft golden Bath stone that had been used to construct most of the buildings suggested they had reached the very end of the rainbow that had arched over Dunstanbury.

The carriage rolled to a stop on a street that ran parallel to the river. Other carriages had already been emptied, and she could see many of the guests from Fortenbury Park milling on the streets. They were admiring items in store windows and discussing where they wished to go first.

As if he were privy to her thoughts, Rupert asked as he handed Aunt Millicent from the carriage, "Where would you like to go first, ladies?"

Aunt Millicent looked back at Rosie and smiled. "Let's walk along the river in the direction of the

Pump Room. Rosie should have to endure the taste of that water at least once during her visit here."

"An excellent idea, as long as I can avoid drinking some of it myself." He held up his hand again to Rosie.

"Is it so terrible?" she asked as she put her fingers on it.

"You must judge for yourself." He chuckled. "It is said to be very good for one's health, but it makes me rather queasy."

Rosie laughed as she stepped down from the carriage. When she reached to adjust her bonnet, which had been jostled during their ride, he did not release her hand. She was about to remonstrate, then realized she could not scold him for being so brazen when they stood on a public street. Instead, she tried to pull her hand out of his.

He smiled broadly and did not release it. His raised brows dared her to make the very scene she wished to avoid.

Although she wanted to demand that he explain why he was acting with such an uncustomary lack of polish, she said nothing. He drew her hand within his arm as he had in the field by the wall. Then he reached up and adjusted the brim of her bonnet as if he were her father. The amazing sensation left by the chance touch of his fingers against her cheek was not in the least daughterly.

"There," he said in not much more than a whisper.

"Thank you." Was her voice as breathless as his sounded? Or mayhap he was calm, and her ears were playing her false because she was so unsettled by the enchantment she could not govern.

"A good host tends to all his guest's needs. A very wise person once told me that."

"Is that so?" She could not resist a laugh at his jesting. And why should she? The day was lovely, and she was about to explore a city that she had heard much about. That thought lightened her steps as she went with Rupert and Aunt Millicent toward the low wall on the other side of the street.

Rosie smiled when she saw the green park set below the wall and edging the Avon. Flowers still filled all the beds, refusing to give up their summer splendor. The grass looked as smooth as velvet. A few people were wandering through the park, and one waved at them. She waved back, thrilled to be part of an excursion that seemed to be out of one of the stories her sister, Bianca, had told by the fire on stormy nights.

"What a lovely park!" she exclaimed.

"The street leading to the bridge is called the Grand Parade, so that is Parade Gardens," Rupert said. "It is truly glorious in the spring when all the flowers are in bloom."

She smiled when her aunt walked a little ways from them to speak with Mrs. Wallace. Aunt Millicent had become very fond of the bride's mother, and Rosie suspected they had met even before the gathering at Henry Jordan's house last month. Although Aunt Millicent usually was forthcoming about everything, she kept her single, interrupted Season much to herself. Rosie was becoming more and more curious why. She did not want to ask her aunt because Aunt Millicent clearly wished Rosie to respect her reticence on this subject, but the curiosity was becoming an exquisite torture.

Pulling her eyes from Aunt Millicent and Mrs. Wallace, Rosie gazed up the river toward the bridge and the weir below it. Again she smiled as she saw the ducks trying to get past the wide steps of the weir.

"They are persistent," she said, pointing to the ducks.

"So is he." Rupert leaned one arm on the wall.

"Who?"

"Yon young boy."

Rosie saw a little boy standing on the other shore, casting in a line. The other children had abandoned their lines, but he still held the makeshift rod. With a laugh, she said, "No doubt he hopes to catch the biggest fish ever to be pulled from the Avon. We used to imagine the incredible behemoths that we would dredge up from the pond behind Dunsworthy Hall."

"Henry and I did much the same when we fished in the water garden. Did you ever catch anything?"

"Not anything that was edible or much bigger than my longest finger. The pond was so shallow that I could wade its breadth even when I was a child."

"Then you did better than we did. There were no fish in the water garden, save for the ornamental ones that Mother had put in there. The gardener kept them so well fed that they had no interest in our hooks."

She laughed again. "Those may have been the only smart fish in the history of the world."

"Just my luck." He turned to see his brother and Jenna walking toward them. Waving, he called, "Come and share our grand fishing tales."

"Fishing tales?" asked Henry.

"I was telling Rosie of our fruitless attempts to catch the ornamental fish Mother kept in the water garden."

Henry's smile broadened. "Not so fruitless. You were off to school the day I went wading in with a butterfly net and captured the lot, tossing them up onto shore."

"Henry!" chided Jenna. "How furious your mother must have been!"

He held up his hand, covered with a fine leather glove. "If you were to look close enough, I'm sure you could see the bruises here still."

Jenna put her hand over his. "I had the opportunity to meet your mother once, and she was a warm-hearted woman. I cannot believe she would have treated you so."

"Save when her fish were left to die on the shore of the pool in the water garden." He roared with laughter.

Rupert clapped his brother on the back, and Rosie could not miss the obvious affection between the brothers. She blinked back sudden tears as they continued along the street.

When an arm curved around her shoulders, she looked up at Rupert in shock. She stiffened, then let her tension vanish as he said, "There is still a chance that your sister and Wandersee will arrive in time for Henry's wedding."

"Am I that transparent?"

"It is not wrong to miss your sister and your brother. I suspect you and your sister and aunt have always been close and became even closer when the three of you moved to the dower cottage."

"That is true. It seems that it has been such a short time since Kevin died, and yet it seems he has been gone so long because he has missed many of the things we used to do together. And I do miss Bianca, even though I am very happy that she is happy." She smiled widely. "There were rumors about Dunstanbury that she was so contrary, no man with his wits about him would ever ask her to marry."

"That shows how accurate rumors are, doesn't it?"

"I try never to heed them. I prefer to judge things for myself."

He grinned at her. "Then I suppose you do not believe the tales of how Bath was a Roman city long before it was an English one."

"That is not a rumor!"

"Even so, I suspect you would like to see the proof for yourself."

Rosie stopped and faced him. A mistake, she realized when he did not withdraw his arm from around her shoulders. Anyone looking at them would think she stood within his embrace.

And she did!

Her thoughts must have been displayed on her face, because he lifted his arm away as his smile wavered. She wanted to apologize, but that would only point out his untoward behavior when he had been intending to offer her solace and friendship.

Forcing her smile back in place, she said in the most cheerful voice she could devise, "I would very much like to see such proof, Rupert."

"Then come with me."

He did not offer his arm, and regret swelled up through Rosie. She had insulted him with her reaction. Again she wished she could find the proper words to apologize. Again the words to do so without offending him refused to come into her head.

"What are we going to see?" she asked.

His smile returned. "You are as curious as a kitten, Rosie."

"That is true." Rosie laughed. When heads along

the street swiveled to stare at her, she lowered her eyes before her heated face could be seen by all the passersby.

"Why are you ashamed of laughing?" Rupert asked, and she knew he had caught sight of her ruddy cheeks.

"I am not ashamed."

"But you are blushing."

She held up her hands to cover her heated face. "I blush at everything."

"I am glad."

"Glad?"

Rupert almost laughed at Rosie's astonishment, but he suspected that would send an even deeper shade of red flying up her cheeks. This woman was such a delightful collection of contradictions. Deeply intelligent and unquestionably naïve, passionate and yet so restrained few would guess she wrote music. She challenged him, but did not pursue him as if he and his title were a prize to be awarded to the most persistent.

He pushed that thought aside. Only Ophelia was annoying him now. Miss Massey had accepted that he offered only his friendship, and she had announced last month her plans to marry a baronet. Miss Hammett quickly found him boring, because he preferred to talk than to dance until he wore holes through the soles of his shoes, which she had done twice, she had told him with pride. And there had been Miss Greenly, who had had no idea where Egypt even was. Both of those misses had made excellent matches, and neither harbored any regret that he had not offered for them. They had written to him to let him know of that and to invite him to their upcoming weddings.

Only Ophelia, whom he had known since the years he spent at Eton, continued to assert that he needed a wife and that wife should be Ophelia King. He had tried to let her know his disinterest in marrying anytime soon in a subtle way so she would turn her attentions to another man. Then he had been much less subtle. He had enlisted Henry's help, and even their mother's brother, Uncle Victor, had offered to assist. The latter gentleman, Rupert believed, had a *tendre* for pretty Ophelia himself. It would have been an outstanding match, but Ophelia would not be budged one bit from her determination that she would persuade Rupert that she must become his wife.

He smiled as Rosie pointed out a street that curved up and away from the river. Her eyes were alight with excitement, an excitement that he had to own he had lost so long ago that he could not recall ever possessing it. He answered her questions and laughed when Henry teased her about her unflagging curiosity.

"You will find Primrose Dunsworthy has a multitude of things she wants to learn about," Rupert said.

"Rupert, please don't use that name!" Rosie chided, exasperated as always when he addressed her by her given name.

He smiled and assumed an expression worthy of a villain upon the stage. "I would gladly do so if you gave me one good reason why I should not."

"I told you. I do not like that name."

"That is not a good reason."

"It is good enough for everyone else."

As his brother and Jenna laughed, Rupert shook his head. "Ask Henry. He will tell you that such a reason has never persuaded me to change my mind."

"It is the only one I can give you today."

"Then I have no choice but to call you Primrose whenever the fancy strikes me."

Jenna interrupted to say, "Take care, Rupert. The fancy may not be the only thing to strike you if you infuriate Rosie. She may choose her words with care, but she uses them well when she chooses to. Such words could be as devastating as a blow."

When they turned the corner toward the Pump Room, he said, "That is a chance I shall have to take . . . Primrose."

She grimaced, much to Henry and Jenna's delight. "If I did not want to see this proof you offered to show me, Rupert, I daresay I would leave you to your own company and your hoaxing."

"Proof?" asked Henry. "Of what?"

"The Roman settlement of Bath."

Henry shook his head. "You have dragged me around too many times to look at dusty old pieces of stone and broken pottery. I will not have another day wasted on the ancient past, and I will not have your long treatises on ruins spoil Jenna's day." He grinned a moment at his sally. "We would rather join the others in the Pump Room for some conversation on topics that deal with matters less than a thousand years old."

As Henry led Jenna along the street, Rupert turned to Rosie. "What I wish to show you is only a few steps beyond the Pump Room."

"Aunt Millicent—"

"And it is right on the street, so you need not worry about being in some dark, dusty hole without a watchdog."

Color flashed up her face. "I did not mean to imply that you would suggest anything untoward."

"I know you did not." He offered his arm.

When she put her fingers on it, he was amazed how warm they were. That gentle heat oozed through her gloves and then through his wool coat and the sleeves of his shirt beneath it to caress his skin like summer sunshine. He looked into her upturned face, and a reaction he should have expected clamped around him. He knew how useless it was to fight the longing. He wanted to pull her closer, so close that he could feel every breath she took. His gaze focused on her lips, which appeared as soft as the underside of a rose petal. How many times had they tempted him? Why was he resisting?

Had he taken a knock in the head while in the cradle? Although he unquestionably enjoyed Rosie's company and she was an endless surprise, unlike many of the women he had met while in London, he liked his life just as it was . . . or just as it would be once the wedding and all its events were past.

Except that with the end of the wedding celebration, Rosie would have returned to Dunsworthy Dower Cottage. He was not astonished how that thought bothered him. What amazed him was the thought that followed right after it: What excuse could he use to convince her to stay awhile longer?

# CHAPTER NINE

Rosie knew she probably should not, but she could not resist reaching out her fingers to touch the stone face. It was part of a bodiless statue leaning against one wall at the end of the street just beyond the Pump Room. The expression was so beautifully carved that she almost expected to discover living flesh beneath her fingers.

She stood slowly. "Thank you for bringing me to see this, Rupert. I doubt you could have found a better example of proof of the Romans settling here. It is beautiful."

"*She* is beautiful."

"Yes, *she* is." Smiling, she was startled when he did not smile back. She wondered if he was somber because they were looking at a Roman artifact. That made no sense, for he had been as happy as a child at play while discussing the Egyptian tablets at his brother's house last month. "Do you think that she is meant to represent a goddess?"

"Most likely so, or mayhap a patroness of the Roman baths that have been here along the river since before recorded history, baths that are connected with the springs here in Bath. Some ruins were discovered here over fifty years ago when the Pump Room was being enlarged, but they were buried again."

"What? Without studying them?"

Finally he smiled, and she guessed some thought that he had not wanted to share had been disturbing him. "Surely you have seen, Primrose—"

"Rupert! If you persist in calling me that, I swear I shall find some way to repay you in kind."

"I am sure you will."

"Something you will not like any more than I like being called by that name."

"And what did you have in mind?"

She was not going to own that she had nothing particular in mind. When they were children, her brother and sister had been the ones who bravely defended the family's honor. She had stood to the side, watching and cheering them on if she thought no one would hear her.

"If I tell you," she said with a laugh, "then it might not seem so horrible."

"Ah, you wish me to put myself into a stew over what you might inflict upon me."

"Now you understand."

"I am forewarned but no more forearmed than this poor creature carved in stone." With a smile as she groaned at his pun, he looked back at the sculptured head. "That there were stones and artifacts like this carved face found around the Pump Room suggests that there may be additional ruins which date back to the time when Britannia was on the frontier of the Roman empire." He looked to where the others were entering the Pump Room. "My friend Mr. Billings has complained over and over that he should open his own pump room because he has that malodorous water seeping into his kitchen and cellars, no matter how he tries to halt it."

"Where does he live?"

"Just around the corner from the Pump Room on the abbey side."

"That might be a good idea. There certainly must be more than one spring close to the Avon. Look how low the river is compared to this street." She laughed. "Do not regard me with such amazement. When one lives as near to the sea as we do in Dunsworthy Dower Cottage, one always keeps track of where the water is and where it might go."

He offered his arm so they might join the others in the Pump Room. "Forgive me. I keep being startled by you because of the assumptions I have come to equate with women and their preferred topics of conversation. I see I am wrong."

"We are not all alike."

"Most definitely."

The sudden tautness of his voice was Rosie's only warning before Miss King appeared out of the crowd and bustled over to them. Boldly, Miss King slipped her hand through Rupert's other arm and tugged on him.

"My dear Rupert," she said in a scolding tone, "I don't know why you wandered away when you must have known how I would be looking for you."

Rosie bit her lip as she waited for Rupert to answer Miss King. The brunette, who was dressed in a beautiful gown of flawless pink, glanced at Rosie, then moved so Rupert could not look at both her and Rosie at the same time. Her coquettish smile did not change, even when she shot Rosie a triumphant look.

"I had no idea that you would be looking for me,

Ophelia," he answered coolly. "You should have sent someone to find me if you needed something."

"Something?" She tapped his arm with her finger as if it were a folded fan. "You silly man! I was not in need of something. I was in need of *someone*—you, who should have joined us posthaste. Everyone else is waiting for you. Why are you being such a laggard when you are our host?"

"I am also Rosie's host, and I was showing her the piece of the antiquated statue dug up from the excavations near the old baths."

Her laugh was as lovely as her gown. "What am I going to do with a man like you whose mind is often lost in the past? It is a good thing that one of us thinks about the future. Come and join us here in the present!" She tugged on him again.

Rosie drew her arm away before she could be dragged after them like a child's kite bumping drearily along the cobbles.

Rupert paused and, acting as if he had not seen Miss King's sudden frown, asked, "Are you coming, Rosie?"

She saw her aunt motioning to her. Her aunt wore a frown almost as grim as Miss King's. No doubt, Aunt Millicent had watched the whole of this ignoble interaction.

Rosie smiled. "If you will excuse me, I need to go and discover what my aunt wishes to say to me. Thank you for showing me the proof, Rupert."

"We will see you inside the Pump Room." He bowed his head toward her before walking away with Miss King.

Rosie sighed. She must not allow Miss King to take away the day's joy. Yet, as she went to where Aunt Millicent was standing beside Mrs. Wallace, the sunshine seemed a bit less warm and the voices along the street not as joyful.

The bride's mother was barely taller than a child, but she had a powerful personality that was behind most of the plans for her daughter's wedding. Aunt Millicent had warned Rosie just last night that the gray-haired Mrs. Wallace was furious with Henry over more than a half dozen things that he had questioned about the wedding breakfast. When she heard how Mrs. Wallace had dressed down her future son-in-law like a judge lecturing a miscreant, Rosie had decided not to do anything that would risk angering Mrs. Wallace.

"There you are," Mrs. Wallace said in her no-nonsense tone. "Your aunt was growing fearful that you had wandered off on your own."

Aunt Millicent hurried to add, "I thought you might be so intrigued with the city that you would want to see it all in one afternoon."

"I do!" Rosie squeezed her aunt's hand, trying to sound as if nothing were amiss. "But just now, I want to see this marvelous Pump Room and try the water that I have heard so much about."

She knew she had tried too hard to appear cheerful when her aunt glanced at her with concern. She struggled to smile. It was no use.

As Mrs. Wallace turned to speak with another of the guests from Fortenbury Park while they streamed in a crowd toward the Pump Room, Aunt Millicent asked quietly, "Are you all right, Rosie?"

"Yes."

"You do not sound all right. Are you distressed?"

"Exasperated would be closer to the truth."

"At Miss—at her?"

Rosie smiled swiftly at her aunt's attempt not to

draw attention to their conversation by speaking Miss King's name. "Yes. Rupert and I were having a pleasant discussion about Roman ruins in Bath. It was impolite of her to intrude."

"And, to own the truth, Rosie, it was impolite for him to go with her."

"He asked me to join them."

Aunt Millicent's eyes widened, then she smiled. As she had when they watched Rupert ride away from Dunsworthy Dower Cottage, she said, "Well."

This time, Rosie was not sure how to reply, so she said nothing as they finally reached the Pump Room door and went in along with the stream of Fortenbury Park guests. Her feet slowed as she stared about herself. She might look like a country bumpkin to be awed, but she did not care as she turned around so she might see everything in the grand room.

The ceiling was high, held up by columns that flanked a large alcove that contained a balcony. Doors topped with pyramids led into other parts of the building. Niches held statues that must be nearly life-sized. Lovely works of art were arranged on the walls.

The far wall was a row of windows set between another row of columns. Over each of the tall windows, an oval window welcomed even more of the sunshine to fall over the guests who filled the room.

In a bay, like a monarch benevolently receiving its subjects, a raised stone urn must have been connected to the spring beneath the building. Water flowed out of its sides and into glasses that were offered to patrons who milled about the room. She took a deep breath, but the air was fresh. Even if the water had a horrible taste, the minerals within it did not flavor the air.

"Shall we?" Aunt Millicent asked, leading Rosie toward the spring.

"I suppose I should."

"A single sip, and you will not have to try it again."

A deeper laugh came from behind her, and, at the delightfully familiar sound, Rosie spun around before she could halt herself. Her heart banged against her chest so hard that she was unsure if she could draw in a breath.

"Rupert! I thought— I mean . . ." She did not want to say what she meant, for it would not be flattering to Miss King.

He took two glasses that were held out to him. "Do try it at least once, Rosie. You may not be glad that you did, but you can brag to your friends that you have done so. I honestly believe that half the people here drink it only for that reason. Its medicinal benefits are at best questionable." He lifted one glass in a salute to her but did not offer her either glass. "Enjoy your sample of the water."

Rosie said nothing as he walked away. What an air-dreamer she had been to think that he had managed to extricate himself from Miss King's company and then had rushed to Rosie's side!

"Here you go," Aunt Millicent said with forced cheerfulness as she came back through the press of people in the room. She held out a glass to Rosie. "I would advise a small sip. That will be best to determine if you can endure to swallow more of it."

Holding up the glass, Rosie took a deep drink. No matter how unsavory the water might be, it could not be more bitter than the unhappiness inside her as she watched Rupert disappear into the crowd in search of Miss King.

Pasting on his best smile, Rupert strode across the Pump Room to where he had left his uncle flirting outrageously with Ophelia. Uncle Victor must have arrived at Fortenbury Park right after they left for Bath. Always enjoying a gathering, Uncle Victor had followed, his coat still fuzzy with the dust from his journey.

Although he was tempted, Rupert did not look back toward the stone urn. He did not want to see Rosie's distress. By thunder! The whole situation was getting more complicated as he tried to be a good host to his brother's wedding guests. He had thought that Rosie was a sensible woman, not one of those clinging, jealous types.

Like Ophelia King.

Rosie had used the slimmest of excuses to rush away and leave him with Ophelia, so he had guessed she was comfortable with him speaking with other women. He was thankful for such a lack of possessiveness, but not as much as he had appreciated how her eyes had glowed with happiness when he spoke with her by the spring's fountain. As he had turned away, he had caught a glimpse of that glow vanishing. Mayhap it was nothing more than she regretted, as he did, how their conversation had been interrupted.

He shook his head in disgust at his own attempts to fool himself. It was not just having their conversation disrupted that annoyed him. He enjoyed Rosie's company, for not only was her intelligent insight a challenge, but he also could speak plainly and not have to worry about every word being mistaken for a marriage proposal. With Ophelia, he had to guard his tongue each time he spoke.

As he reached where Ophelia and his uncle stood by a hearth at one end of the room, Ophelia was responding to Uncle Victor's compliments with coos and coquettish smiles. His uncle was a handsome man in his mid-forties. Never seen without a cane, which he did not need to help him walk, and a stylish hat perched on his silver hair, he could have been mistaken for an ambassador or a butler.

Rupert chuckled at his own bizarre thought. Uncle Victor would not be pleased to learn of either comparison. But his uncle was unquestionably pleased with Ophelia's attentions. Hmmm . . . was this a solution to the problem that had aggravated him beyond words? His uncle had a considerable fortune of his own and a splendid house in London. Both should gladden Ophelia's covetous heart, for she had made several comments already today about how Fortenbury Park was good enough for a country seat, but it could not offer the excitement of a Mayfair house and Town. She did not hide her opinion that Bath was a backwater town, fit only for a short stay on one's way to London.

"Ah, dear boy, here you are at long last!" crowed his uncle. "A man could die of thirst waiting on you."

"It would not have done to splatter water on my brother's future mother-in-law as I passed by her." Rupert handed one glass to his uncle, who took a gulp that drained half of it, and the other to Ophelia.

Her nose wrinkled. "Really, Rupert, I would have thought that you would recall how I loathe this liquid."

"That is true," Uncle Victor said with a broad smile, "for there is little forgettable about a lovely woman like you, Ophelia. How could you be so forgetful, my boy?"

She preened at his praise and refilled his glass from her own. Somehow, she made the motion seem incredibly intimate. "Rupert, your uncle is always such a charmer. He could turn the head of a simple country lass like me."

Rupert was glad that he was not drinking the water, for it would have exploded out of his mouth at her absurd comment. He simply smiled. Mayhap Ophelia had been born in the country, but since that day she had avoided any place where there were not cobbles under her feet. She had been one of the first to reach London at the beginning of the past two Seasons, and she had lingered there even after most of the *ton* had left. Her clothes were unsuitable for the rougher life of the country, and he doubted if she owned a pair of high-lows for walking along a muddy country lane.

He let the rhythm of their voices, parrying like two skilled swordsmen as they flirted openly, flow around him. His mind swept him away from the Pump Room and back to the field beyond Fortenbury Park's knot garden. Anew, he was astonished by how Rosie's voice had been filled with such delight as she sang when she thought nobody else could hear. He had heard, and now he could not help noticing that every motion she made, every word she spoke seemed to contain that same music. It had surrounded him and seemed to seep within him in a silent invitation to be part of her song. He never had experienced anything like this, and it intrigued him.

"Oh, Miss Dunsworthy, do not hurry past!" called Ophelia's voice.

Rupert frowned as Rosie halted and turned, an

expression of dismay appearing on her face before she could mask it. Rosie had not fooled him outside on the street. Her aunt's motion had given her an excuse to leave Ophelia's company, which she clearly found disconcerting. He understood all too well, and he had acquiesced into going with Ophelia to prevent Rosie from suffering from the ofttimes honed edge of her tongue.

"Yes, Miss King?" Rosie asked.

"Do come and speak with us!"

"I am afraid I already promised Henry and Jenna that I would join them by the windows."

Ophelia laughed lightly. "They will not mind a few extra minutes alone to speak about all the important things that lovers discuss." She slipped her right hand through the crook of Rupert's arm as she had on the street. "Isn't that true, Rupert, my dear?"

Rosie stiffened but hoped her strained smile would cover her thoughts. Looking past Ophelia, she recognized the man standing to her left. She had met him only briefly in Plymouth.

"Mr. Byrne, good afternoon," she murmured.

"Why, if it isn't Miss Primrose Dunsworthy!" He surged forward and took her hand. Bowing over it, he raised it to his lips. When she drew it out of his before he could kiss it, he chuckled. "It is a pleasure to see you again, Miss Dunsworthy. A true pleasure, if I may say so. A true pleasure, indeed."

"Thank you." She was unsure how else to reply. Mr. Byrne's effusive welcome threatened to undo her vow not to hide herself in her usual bashful cocoon while at the Pump Room. She had thought it would be an easy pledge to fulfill because all the others in the room seemed intent in conversations that did not include her.

"Ophelia," Mr. Byrne said, barely pausing as words gushed from him like water from the stone urn, "you spoke Miss Dunsworthy's name, so I can see you two have been introduced before I could have the opportunity to do so."

"Dear Rupert did the honors when Miss Dunsworthy and her aunt arrived at Fortenbury Park."

"Rupert, eh?" Mr. Byrne chuckled. "Yes, I do recall you being quite taken by Miss Dunsworthy at Jordan Court, my boy. Danced quite a few dances with her, you did, if I remember correctly." He winked at his nephew. "And I believe I do."

Miss King's mouth tightened into a caricature of her usual smile as Mr. Byrne continued with his prattle. Was he trying to infuriate Miss King? If so, he was succeeding. Rosie longed for a way—any way—to escape. Her aunt was busy speaking again to Mrs. Wallace and the other ladies who were gathered near the street door. Jenna and Henry were lost in their world of love by the window. Neither her aunt nor the betrothed couple were close enough to offer her an excuse to leave.

"Uncle Victor," Rupert said, interrupting Mr. Byrne in the midst of a word, "if you continue to recite every detail of the weekend at Henry's house, we shall stand here for another weekend to relive it."

"Yes," seconded Miss King. She gave Rosie a baleful glower but was smiling warmly when she looked up at Rupert. "I believe *we* have kept Miss Dunsworthy long enough at our sides when she wishes to go and join your brother and his intended."

"If you will excuse me . . ." Rosie had not guessed that Miss King would offer her the very pretext she needed to flee from this uncomfortable conversation.

"Nonsense!" Mr. Byrne did not hide his frown at

Miss King. "Do not banish her. *I* am enjoying Miss Dunsworthy's conversation."

Miss King chuckled. "Conversation? She has not said a score of words. If you do have something to say, please say it posthaste, Miss Dunsworthy."

"Ophelia, do not tease her." Rupert's voice remained low.

"I am trying to *help* her. No one is going to make an offer for a meek lamb who does not say muff." Her gaze flicked along Rosie from head to foot as her smile broadened. "The dear *child* surely must be grateful for every bit of advice she can receive."

Rosie knew she should say something, but the words she wanted to speak must remain unuttered. As Miss King pressed her full breasts to Rupert's arm, there was no doubt that Miss King considered Rupert hers and hers alone. He edged aside a halfstep, but Miss King continued to cling to his arm as if it were a part of her own body.

"Aren't you grateful, Miss Dunsworthy?" persisted Miss King, ignoring Rupert's request to hold her tongue.

"I am grateful." She faltered, then said, "I am grateful to all with vastly more experience than I have who help me out of the goodness of their hearts."

Mr. Byrne roared with laughter. Downing the rest of the water in his glass, he set it on a nearby mantel. "Goodness of one's heart? Vastly more experience? Dear Ophelia, did you hear that? The dear *child* clearly has some wit about her."

"Excuse me," Rosie said, backing away before Miss King could voice the thoughts in her blazing eyes. When she bumped into a matron who was scowling at her as fiercely as Miss King was, she turned and sought some haven among the anonymity of the crowd.

Was that Rupert speaking her name? She glanced over her shoulder, but Miss King was speaking earnestly to him, her hand still on his arm. Anyone looking at the two of them would guess another announcement of a wedding forthcoming from Fortenbury Park soon.

Rosie told herself that she should be glad that she and Aunt Millicent were staying only a few more days in Bath. The game of insults that were disguised as pleasant conversation was one Miss King played with such obvious ease. Rosie did not want to learn it. Not ever. Had Aunt Millicent turned her back on the Polite World for this very reason? Rosie had never considered *that* before, for she had been enrapt with the fairy tales her sister had told of dashing heroes and elegant ladies who lost their hearts to each other in the midst of a dance. The reality of the *ton* was much different.

With a grimace, she set her glass on a table where no one was sitting. She had forgotten she was still carrying it about. Mayhap it was just as well, because the temptation to fling its contents in Miss King's face might have been too great to ignore. What was she thinking? She had been raised to have better manners than to throw water into someone's face in the Pump Room. But Miss King made her so angry!

Suddenly the room seemed too close, and the conversation could be described only as a buzz in her ears. Was she about to swoon? Dear heavens, she had never swooned.

"Are you all right?" asked Aunt Millicent from near Rosie's left elbow.

"I think some fresh air might be advisable." She put her hand on her stomach, which abruptly ached.

"You are the gray of old snow." Aunt Millicent steered her toward the door. "Did the water from the spring upset your stomach, or is it something else?"

"I guess I should not have swallowed so much of it." She hated being less than completely honest with her aunt, because she suspected her unusually high emotions were at least partly to blame for her light head. There was no time to debate the truth, for she needed to get out of the Pump Room before she embarrassed herself.

Stepping out of the busy room into the street, which seemed just as clogged, Rosie was glad when her aunt led her quickly through the press of people and along Stall Street, which was less crowded. She took steadying breaths, paying no mind to the merchandise displayed in the shop windows.

"Better?" asked Aunt Millicent.

"I believe so." She managed to smile as the shops gave way to homes. With their flat fronts and identical windows, she wondered how often someone entered the wrong house. The peculiar thought was a sign she was regaining both her mental and her physical equilibrium.

"Have you been enjoying yourself?"

At the pointed question, Rosie glanced at her aunt and away before she could say the wrong thing. Not the wrong thing, but the truth. She knew what Aunt Millicent wanted to know, because her aunt was worried about her. But, for the first time in her life, Rosie was unwilling to answer such a question. Instead, she replied, "I find it difficult to believe I am here where the *ton* has walked since the last century."

"And played." Aunt Millicent smiled at a building in front of them, and Rosie guessed her aunt was placated with an answer that was a part of the truth. "There is the Theater Royal."

Rosie was not certain what she expected a theater in Bath to look like, but this building resembled the houses on either side of it. Made of the same golden stone, it had identical windows. A stone railing at the roofline was unique, as were the letters announcing what it was.

"I wonder what is playing there," Aunt Millicent mused.

"There is a woman over there sweeping the walkway," Rosie said. "Mayhap she knows."

Aunt Millicent smiled, patting Rosie's hand. Did her aunt guess that Rosie was seeking any way to postpone their return to the Pump Room? Seeing Miss King draping herself over Rupert like a cyprian was something she did not want to view again.

Unlike her, Aunt Millicent was not reluctant to speak to a stranger. She went to where the gray-haired woman was sweeping dirt and droppings into the gutter.

"Good day," Aunt Millicent said.

"Good day to you." The round woman paused in her work and leaned on the handle of the broom. "'Tis the perfect day for a bit of cleaning before the cold comes."

"Yes, it is. Do you live in this house?"

The woman hooked a thumb toward the house set next to the theater. She smiled and shook her head. "That was Mr. Nash's house, the one he built for himself after he designed all the finest parts of this city. I live in the one neighboring it, but I clean up the walkway here as well."

"Mr. Nash's house?" Aunt Millicent smiled at Rosie

to include her in the conversation. "Imagine that! I have been admiring his work during our stroll."

"He and his mistress, Julianna Popjoy, lived here for many years." The woman clearly was pleased to have an audience to share old gossip with. "It is said that Julianna Popjoy's ghost still wanders these streets and throughout this house that she loved."

"And Mr. Nash's ghost?"

The round woman laughed. "I suspect his ghost remains very near hers. They were quite inseparable when they lived here. She was deeply devoted to him, as I believe he was to her."

"Can you tell us what is playing at the theater?"

The woman glanced at the theater and shrugged. "Usually they have a board out front to show what play is being performed. If you come back later, it might be out." She continued to sweep the walkway in front of the house, moving in the direction of the theater.

"What a lovely story," Aunt Millicent mused as she and Rosie continued along the street, "like one of the tales you always have liked hearing Bianca tell on a cold and windy night."

"I shall have to share this one with her." Rosie glanced into the shop windows now that she was not blinded with her own dismay. "I am sure she will embellish it with even grander happenings."

"And a happy-ever-after ending."

"Always."

"The same happy-ever-after ending that you want for yourself."

Rosie continued to gaze into the windows, but once again the merchandise blurred into a confusion of colors as she sought a way to answer without upsetting her aunt. "I think that is something that each one of us wants."

"Ophelia King most definitely does."

"I would prefer not to speak of her."

"But I would," Aunt Millicent said, shocking Rosie, for she had not guessed her aunt would wish to discuss Miss King while they were in public, where anyone might hear.

"Why? I am trying to put her out of my mind."

Aunt Millicent stormed past her, then stood in the middle of the walkway, facing her. With arms folded in front of her, Aunt Millicent said, "You have always avoided confrontation, Rosie. You always chose to let your sister and your brother fight your battles for you. But Kevin is dead, and your sister now has a life of her own where she cannot be with you to protect you whenever you find yourself in a situation you want to escape."

"Why are you saying these horrible things?"

"Horrible? Only if you believe the truth is horrible, and mayhap you do, for you have avoided speaking much of it to me of late. I never expected to discover from someone else that you were again writing words to music."

"I would have told you when . . ."

"When? When the song was finished?" Aunt Millicent shook her head. "Rosie, you cannot choose when you wish to shut everyone out and when you are willing to let them in. Shutting the whole world and its brother out because you fear you will be hurt or embarrass yourself is impossible."

"Don't you understand? It is not just myself I am afraid of embarrassing! It is you."

Her aunt's voice softened. "I know that, Rosie, and I know as well that it is high time these things were said between us. You know it is true that you have learned to depend on Bianca to protect you from disagreeable situations." Lowering her arms from her stern pose, Aunt Millicent said, "Now you must deal with them yourself. I know you wish to, for I have seen how you glow like a star in the night sky when Rupert is near."

"I like his company."

"So does Miss King."

Rosie stepped around her aunt and continued along the street. Talking about Miss King was useless. When her aunt caught up with her, she said much the same.

"Nonsense," Aunt Millicent retorted.

"It *is* nonsense."

"No, *you* are full of nonsense."

Whirling, Rosie faced her aunt. "You seem to be forgetting one important facet of all this. Rupert can speak with whom he pleases whenever he pleases."

"But he is not pleased to speak with Miss King."

"Then why does he speak with her so often?" Her voice came out in a near sob. She pressed her fingers to her lips to keep another from escaping.

"I cannot answer that for you. The only one who can is Rupert. I think it is time you posed that very question to him."

"I cannot!"

Aunt Millicent's eyes filled with tears. "But you must, Rosie, if you wish to save him from Miss King's plans to become Lady Rupert Fortenbury."

"Me? Save him?" She shook her head. "You are exaggerating, Aunt Millicent. This is not an Arthurian legend, and I am certainly no all-powerful heroine who can rush in and sweep Miss King out of Rupert's way as easily as that woman was sweeping the street."

"Out of his way? I would say rather out of *your* way. It is clear to me that you prefer his company to anyone else's at Fortenbury Park."

"I am comfortable speaking with him. It is no more than that."

"It isn't? Are you sure?"

"I am," Rosie said, although she was not. She liked Rupert. She liked him a lot, for he shared her interests in ancient history and her delight in attempting to solve the puzzle of the Egyptian symbols. And, more important than that, she had discovered today that he admired her music.

"Is it all *he* wants?" Aunt Millicent persisted.

"I don't know."

"Then I think you must speak with him right away, Rosie."

"Speak with him of *this*?"

Aunt Millicent nodded. "You have been fortunate, until now, that your bashful ways have not stolen anything of import from you. However, unless you speak your mind—and your heart—this time, Rosie, I believe you will learn how necessary it is that you speak up for what you want before it is lost."

"I cannot speak to him of this." She raised her hands and shrugged. "How can I speak to him of this when I am not even certain of my feelings about—about—?"

"About him?"

"About everything!"

"Then, my dearest Rosie, I fear that if you do nothing you will lose every chance to speak with him. Miss King will most assuredly guarantee you do not . . . ever again."

# CHAPTER TEN

Rupert knew exactly where to find Millicent Dunsworthy. Each morning, she took a walk in the formal garden, which received the day's first sunlight. He was unsure if she went there because she enjoyed the garden or because, as he did, she despaired of ever having a moment alone to think with so many guests crowding the usually serene corridors of Fortenbury Park. Apparently Henry had invited the whole of the Polite World—or mayhap the whole world—to the wedding, and everyone had accepted.

On his short journey from the stairs to the door opening on the eastern side of the house, four people had halted him, needing to ask him about the location of a certain room or the best place to shop for a gift in Bath. He had given each of them a quick answer in a cheerful voice that suggested he had nothing else to consider but his position as their host. Each request tried his patience more, but he held on to his temper and made his escape from the house.

The dew was heavy on the grass, and he was glad he had worn his riding boots. A breeze whispered through the branches, and he heard the distinct sound of the leaves, which were drying and losing their supple motions along with their color. The rattle was a reminder of how soon winter would be sweeping down upon Fortenbury Park, bringing early nights and slow dawns. By then, Henry and Jenna would be settled in their home at Jordan Court near Plymouth, and he could concentrate on his studies both here and in distant Egypt. He knew many others in England and on the Continent were searching for an answer to the secret to the Egyptian writing. Someone would find it. Of that, he was certain. As soon as that happened, whether he found the clue to decipher the symbols or someone else did, he would redouble his studies in an effort to learn to read those taunting symbols on those tablets.

"Good morning, Rupert."

He shaded his eyes and looked over a low hedge to discover that Millicent had seen him before he had seen her. She was dressed in a blue gown that flattered her coloring, and he wondered anew why this lovely woman had not wed. Surely there must have been a man who could overlook the fact that she was responsible for her nephew and nieces.

"I had hoped to find you here," he replied, seeing no reason not to be honest.

"I am not surprised."

He smiled. He respected the candor the Dunsworthy women had shown him.

"What do you wish to speak to me about?" she asked, then laughed. "That is a silly question, I am sure. You wish to speak to me about Rosie."

"Yes." All at once, he felt as if he stood in front of his tutor and was about to confess to some horrible misdemeanor. Shaking aside that nonsensical thought, he motioned toward a stone bench set underneath a nearby oak. "Shall we sit?"

She shook her head. "I would prefer to walk as we talk, if you do not mind. I fear I shall spend the rest of the day sitting with one of your guests or another while we talk. Such idleness is not customary for me, and I find it difficult to remain seated all day."

"If you wish to ride, there are horses in the stable for my guests."

"Ride?" Her eyes brightened. "Rosie loves to ride, and she has not had an occasion to do so since . . ."

"Since you gave up your place as chatelaine of Dunsworthy Hall." Walking with her along the path made of small stones, he said, "It seems she has given up far too much since you moved to Dunsworthy Hall."

"What do you mean?"

"First of all, I meant no insult to you." He took a deep breath, then said, "I told you how I chanced upon Rosie singing a song of her own composition. She has a true gift for music."

"Yes, she does." Millicent clasped her hands. "Rosie has always been the quietest of my brother's children, mayhap because she always had Kevin and Bianca to speak for her."

"Or mayhap because her mind was focused on her music."

"*Her* music? You have no idea how close you are to the truth, Rupert. She thought she was keeping the truth a secret from me, but I know she had begun to write her own music, the music she said always played within her mind, just before Kevin bought his commission and left for the Continent. I thought she had set it aside completely until I heard you speak of it." Tears filled her eyes. "Kevin's death was a double tragedy for Rosie, for, in her music, she found a way to express herself that has often been difficult for her to do with words beyond her family." Her smile reappeared. "And except with you, I must own. She seems far more comfortable with you than I have seen her with anyone outside of Dunstanbury."

"Yes, she seemed quite ready to give your constable a scold when he threatened to arrest Moss for driving too quickly through the village."

"Did she?"

"You sound astonished."

"I am. She has been bashful around Constable Powers since he first expressed his interest in calling upon her."

Rupert kept his smile in place, but his gut ached as if someone had driven a fist into its very center. When Millicent glanced at him, clearly waiting for him to answer, he said, "The constable made his interest clear when he called at the cottage the night I arrived."

"Davis Powers was my nephew's good friend, and he became Rosie's friend as well when she was quite young. Dunstanbury is so small that we do not let the differences in class keep the children from playing together. He is a very nice young man, quite dedicated to his work and well-respected throughout the shire."

"I am sure he is, for he seems to have many people willing to help him in the recovery of the stolen horses."

"But?"

He regarded her with a smile. "I do not believe I said but."

"Yet, I heard it."

"I collect you did." He would not offend her. She was being completely honest, and he could not be less than the same himself. "I am sure Constable Powers is well-respected far beyond the boundaries of Dunstanbury, but I do not believe Rosie views him as someone other than her brother's friend."

Millicent laughed softly. "You have clear-seeing eyes."

"No, it is nothing more than she defended Moss so thoroughly."

"And defended you as well, I suspect."

"That is true." It was his turn to chuckle. If Uncle Victor was interested in a match instead of simply a flirtation, Rupert would not have hesitated to suggest that his uncle be Millicent's partner at the wedding breakfast. As it was, he would not afflict this kind lady with his raffish uncle. "I believe the good constable would have been happy to toss both me and Moss into his jail for crimes that we did not commit."

"But you did commit a crime."

"What? I assure you, Millicent, that neither Moss nor I were traveling at a speed that would have endangered anyone in Dunstanbury."

She laughed and, bending, picked a white chrysanthemum. She handed it to him. "Think upon this, Rupert."

"This white flower?"

"Which is a symbol of truth." She smiled, revealing a dimple in her right cheek that he had not noticed before. "As you and Rosie like to study old artifacts, I enjoy the study of the language of flowers. This flower symbolizes truth, and I believe it is something that you should consider."

"I assure you that I have not been dishonest with either you or Rosie."

"I speak of honesty with oneself, Rupert. If you will be forthright with yourself, you will know that I believe no more than you do that Constable Powers wished to send you off for a quarter stretch in jail simply because of the speed you were traveling." She patted his arm. "He wished to ensure that he has no rivals for Rosie's attention." She nodded to him. "Good morning, Rupert."

He did not follow when she continued on her walk about the garden. Looking down at the blossom he held, he tossed it back onto the grass. By thunder! He had not expected, when he came here to apologize to Millicent for allowing Ophelia to divert him from his duties as a good host yesterday in Bath, that Millicent would speak frankly about her niece. Mayhap the Dunsworthy women's candor was not such a good thing, after all. He needed no warmhearted aunt with the best of intentions trying to make a match for him with her niece. It was bad enough that Ophelia was using every opportunity to remind him that she would make him a good wife.

His curse was spoken low enough so it would not reach Millicent's ears. He hoped he had convinced Ophelia last evening in this very garden that she should turn her eyes on some other man in her quest for a husband. By thunder! He had not expected her to kiss him. When she had told him that she was tired of waiting for him to kiss *her*, he had extricated himself from the conversation much more smoothly than he had from her embrace.

Rupert went back into the house, heading for his book-room as he had last night. It was now his lone sanctuary in Fortenbury Park.

The room was not large, and every flat surface was covered with open books and magnifying glasses and samples of the stone tablets that had come from Egypt. Even the windowsills of the two bay windows flanking a hearth supported stacks of books. The shelves against the opposite wall were overflowing with books. Once Henry was wed and the house quiet once more, Rupert planned to have more shelves built to hold the books he had purchased on recent visits to London.

Sitting at his dark walnut desk, which, like everything else in the room, was ajumble with books, he reached for one of the fragments that he had been meaning to examine again after reading the MacDonald book a third time. The door opened without so much as the courtesy of a knock.

"Uncle Victor," he said, not standing, "I did not expect to see you up at this early hour."

Moving some books to the floor, his uncle sat in Rupert's favorite chair by the wide bay window that offered the best view of the hot garden. The flowers, all in shades of red and orange, were drooping, their color usurped by the autumn leaves.

But Uncle Victor paid the garden no mind. Nor did he look at any of the books filling the shelves or the fragments of tablets lined up neatly on Rupert's desk. He sat in the comfortable green chair and put his feet up on the stool as he folded his hands across the blue brocade front of his waistcoat.

"My boy," his uncle said, "I am about to say what I never thought I would have to say to you. Your brother, most definitely, but you never."

"And what do you wish to say to me?"

"You are a widgeon. A beautiful woman like that, and you do not want her kisses? What is wrong with you?"

"I am surprised that Ophelia rushed to you with such speed to speak of the matter." Truthfully, he was not, but he could not accuse his uncle of abetting Ophelia in her efforts to persuade Rupert to marry her.

His uncle gave a sigh worthy of an actor on the stage. "I happened upon her when she was piping her eyes upstairs. The poor child was distressed nearly beyond words."

"Nearly."

"Yes!" Uncle Victor sat straighter in the chair. "If I had such a lass in honest pursuit of me, I would be an extremely happy man."

"You would be."

"But you are not. And why not?"

"Uncle Victor, I will not discuss Ophelia in this manner. It is not befitting of gentlemen to speak of a lady thusly."

His uncle snorted like a bull pawing the ground and readying to charge. "Gentlemen discuss women all the time, ladies or not. That you would know if you pulled your head out of the past and looked around yourself."

"I assure you, Uncle, that I am not lost in the past." What would his uncle say if Rupert owned that many of his thoughts were focused on Rosie?

"Then there must be a reason why you spurn Ophelia's most obvious charms."

"I have no wish to lead her down a garden path when I have no intention of paying address to her."

Uncle Victor snorted again. "My boy, I admired your father greatly. He was a good and intelligent man, but he clearly failed in your education when it came to the subject of women. I said nothing about leg-shackling yourself to Ophelia King. I was speaking of other things."

"Then, Uncle, you insult her as well as me. Ophelia is not a light-skirt eager for a tumble and whatever bauble might be tossed in her direction. I would not deign to treat her so."

"This self-righteous attitude is annoying." He drew a cigar out from beneath his coat. Lighting it, he puffed smoke, sending clouds about the room. "I had hoped you would grow to be less like my brother-in-law. You are like him in so many ways. Just like him, you have been too studious and focused on the duties you inherited along with your title. It seems he gave you his self-righteousness as a bequest, too." His eyes narrowed as a smile edged along his lips. "Now that I think of it, he always acted this way when he had something he wanted to hide behind that cold barrier. I can only assume that you are doing the same."

"You may assume whatever you wish, but I am done discussing Ophelia."

"Good. Then we shall discuss Primrose Dunsworthy."

Rupert shook his head as he set the fragment back in its place on his desk. While Uncle Victor was in the mood for a conversation, Rupert was not going to have a chance to compare it to what had been written in the book.

"Speaking of her would only serve to prove that we are below reproach," he replied.

"Aha!"

"Do not 'aha' me, Uncle Victor." He chuckled. "I know you wish to believe you have stumbled upon some great conspiracy to keep you uninformed about matters of my private life, but there is none."

"But you do not wish to speak of this young lady."

"Or any other. I wish to check the validity of an item I recently read."

"You are becoming a dead bore, my boy."

He chuckled. "I am just as I always have been. You simply are without anyone else at the moment to share some bibble-babble."

His uncle puffed up like a bud about to burst, but a knock on the door halted him from venting what he had to say. With relief, Rupert called for whoever was on the far side to enter.

"Ah, here you are," Henry said as he walked over to where his uncle was sitting. He patted Uncle Victor on the shoulder and then faced Rupert. "Just the two I wanted to see."

"And what advice can we offer the groom-to-be this morning, my boy?" Uncle Victor asked. "What is it that two old bachelors can share with a young chap like you who is about to take that eternal walk to the altar?"

Henry dropped heavily onto the settee in front of the bookcases. Draping himself across the cushions, he paid no attention to the books that fell onto the floor. He stared at the ceiling and lamented, "I am a leather-head."

Rupert came to his feet and around his desk. "Why are you a fool this time?"

"I should never have allowed Jenna to persuade me to marry in September."

"And why is that?"

"The month is way too short. I should have agreed to marry in a longer month."

Rupert laughed. "You are fretting like an old tough watching after a young miss. You know you have been anticipating this ceremony as eagerly as Jenna has."

"And the honeymoon to follow," tossed in Uncle Victor.

"Mayhap," Henry said, sitting up with an abrupt grin, "I should have arranged to marry in February."

"Now you *are* a leather-head," Uncle Victor said. "As one far older than you, I can assure you that the march of days goes by at the same pace in every month. By the way, Rupert, don't you have something in this dusty room to satisfy the palate?"

Yet another knock sounded at the door. Wanting to banish everyone so he could have some time to satisfy his curiosity about the fragment, Rupert called for the person to come in. The house was getting too crowded, he decided, as the door to his book-room opened *again*.

As if on cue—which he suspiciously guessed was quite right—Ophelia came in with a tray. She never would have run a servant's errands unless she had an ulterior motive. He suspected that she was eager to be part of this conversation, although he was unsure why. Ophelia would not truly care if they spoke of her when she was not present. She *would* be distressed if they failed to speak of her.

Holding out the tray, which was topped by a bottle of Rupert's best brandy and several glasses, she sashayed across the room. She set the tray on the desk, brushing against Rupert so lightly that he would be a cad to accuse her of being brazen. The glance she flashed was not a come-hither glance. It was more of a here-and-now glance.

He did not let his laugh escape. What would she do if some man were to act on that blatant invitation? He would not be the man to find out, because that would create an endless imbroglio.

When Rupert did not move, Ophelia pouted before turning to Uncle Victor. "I thought you would like this," she murmured, giving his uncle the smile that always brought an answering smile from Uncle Victor.

"We like anything you have, my dear."

Rupert swallowed his groan. Why were these two acting as if they were caught up in the world's most insipid calf-love? His brother was shuffling his feet, abruptly appearing as if he wished to be anywhere—even the altar—than here. Did Ophelia hope to arouse Rupert's passions by flirting with his uncle? Or was she hoping to get Uncle Victor to propose if Rupert continued to pretend to ignore her suggestions of marriage?

Although Uncle Victor owned to being a couple of decades older than Ophelia, he would keep her on her toes. *Although on her toes is not where she is aiming to be with that smile,* Rupert groused silently. Pouring brandy, he handed a glass to his brother.

Henry arched one eyebrow, and Rupert found it even more difficult not to laugh. He offered another glass to his uncle.

"Ophelia?" he asked, holding up the bottle.

"Do not be silly! I am on my way to sit with Jenna during her final fitting." Her voice softened to a purr as she added, "But thank you for the offer, Rupert, my dear."

"Who would have guessed that you would turn down any offer from Rupert at this late date?" asked Uncle Victor before taking another sip of his brandy.

Rupert waited for Ophelia to bristle, but she did not. That surprised him, for she was usually as volatile as gunpowder.

"Oh, Victor, you are such a jester!" She patted his shoulder.

As Ophelia swayed to the door, Uncle Victor blew

a kiss to her. She made a grand show of catching it, but smiled at Rupert. He waited until she closed the door, then he sighed. This was going to be a very long weekend.


Rosie thanked the maid who had led her to Jenna Wallace's door. The request for Rosie to come here had arrived just as she was beginning another of Rupert's books, but she had set the book aside to follow the maid. She had been trying to read the same three paragraphs for the past hour with little success. It was as if the book itself were written in the forgotten Egyptian hieroglyphics, for she had not comprehended a single word, in spite of reading them over and over.

She understood what each word said, but the meaning refused to stick in her brain. Mayhap it was because her mind was whirling with so many thoughts already. *Now*, almost a day after the trip into Bath, she could think only of the sharp retorts she could have given Ophelia yesterday. At the time, when they stood in the Pump Room, she had halted herself from speaking each one. That was the proper thing to do, and, even though Ophelia was clearly eager to shatter the boundaries of polite conversation, Rosie was not.

The door opened before Rosie could knock, and she was ushered into a sitting room decorated in white and gilt. It reminded her of the grand ballroom at Jordan Court, but she had to own that she preferred the bedchamber she was using here. Her room might not be as large, but the deep reds and soft greens of the upholstery suggested she was in the midst of a walk through an autumn forest.

"This way, Miss Dunsworthy," the maid said.

Rosie followed the slight girl to a door that led into what must have been the largest dressing room Rosie had ever seen or even imagined. It was so big that it had a window. Lace curtains were pulled over the panes to offer some privacy, although no one would be able to peek into a room two stories above the ground.

One woman was kneeling on the floor, her mouth looking as if she had bitten onto a hedgehog. She looked up, then bent to her work again as she removed a pin she was holding between her teeth and stuck it expertly into the gown on the other woman, who was trying not to move.

Jenna stood on a stool, but she looked every inch the perfect bride. Her brown hair falling down her back and curling along her shoulders contrasted with the pristine white of her gown. Lace of the same color edged the bodice and the sleeves. Pearls had been sewn into a pattern along the skirt. The silk glistened primly in the light from the window and whispered when Jenna turned to look over her shoulder.

"Just the person I had hoped to see," Jenna said as she waved for Rosie to come closer. "Shut the door and help me decide if I want one row of ruffles on the bottom of my gown or two."

A seamstress glanced up again around the bottom of Jenna's gown, clearly curious who was being asked such a question. She appeared to be younger than Rosie, but her fingers moved with skill and speed as she pinned a single ruffle along the hem.

"Me?" asked Rosie. "I have no idea what is *de rigueur* in Town this year."

"Which is why I would like your opinion. Others

will fall back on what the fashion-plates deem to be proper. I can trust you to tell me what you think looks best. You are not prejudiced by what others have worn." Her joyous laugh was almost a song. "After all, this will be my single chance to be a bride, and I believe I should look my very best on this day."

"So you should be the one who sets the style on your special day."

"Exactly!" Jenna clapped her hands, then dropped them back to her sides as the *modiste* warned her not to move. "What do you think?"

Rosie smiled. This decision was simple, and if Jenna had not been constrained by what was *à la modality*, she would have known herself.

"A single ruffle," Rosie replied. "Not only are you tiny and could be overmastered by a double ruffle, but two ruffles will draw attention to them and away from you."

"Oh, thank you! I knew you would be sensible about the whole of this. Henry is right."

"About what?"

"He says you are the most sensible woman he has ever met. You know when to speak and when to keep your tongue between your teeth. You do not make demands or flirt outrageously like—" She put one hand over her mouth, then dropped it back to her side as the seamstress frowned at her again. "I am sorry, Rosie."

"You have no reason to apologize to *me*."

Jenna laughed. "Do stay and talk with me. These fittings are filling me with *ennui*."

Rosie sat in a chair by the window and waited while the seamstress finished her work. The woman helped Jenna remove the dress, which was prickly with pins. As Jenna redressed, Rosie began to button up the back.

As soon as the seamstress took her leave, Jenna whirled to face Rosie, even though some of the buttons remained undone. "I do owe you an apology, Rosie, although you are gracious not to chide me in front of my *modiste*. I should not have compared you to anyone else."

"You were only saying what you thought. The truth may be difficult, but it is the truth."

"You are very generous-hearted not to add to the demure hits I made to Ophelia King. I have seen how she has cut you direct whenever she can."

"Turn about, so I can get these last few buttons." As she finished closing Jenna's gown, Rosie added, "I do not let Ophelia bother me."

"Balderdash!"

Rosie chuckled. "All right, you are right. I *try* not to let her bother me."

"But she does bother you."

"I have never met anyone who seems so determined to undermine others in order to build herself up in someone's eyes."

"Not just someone. Rupert." Taking Rosie by the arm, Jenna took a piece of ribbon from an open drawer. Then she steered Rosie back out into the antechamber. She sat on a gold settee and motioned for Rosie to sit beside her. "For as long as I have known Rupert, Ophelia has been a bothersome gnat to any woman he has spoken to more than once, always buzzing about and making a nuisance of herself until the other woman just gives in and goes away."

"I am glad to know it is not something I have done that irks her."

"You?" Jenna laughed as she drew back her hair and looped the ribbon around it. "It is most definitely you who has unsettled her. She is furious that you share Rupert's interest in his dreary slabs of stone."

"They are not dreary!"

"See?" Jenna smiled broadly. "You jump to his defense, just as I knew you would. As Ophelia knows you would. That is why she is intent on making you miserable. She succeeded at the Pump Room, I am sorry to say. If I had had any idea of what she was doing—"

"You were busy, and she is my problem. You need to think only of your wedding."

"My wedding must not come at the expense of my newest friend."

Rosie smiled at Jenna's warm words. "It will not. I promise you. I will try not to let her succeed in belittling me again."

"Good!" Tying her hair ribbon with a flourish, Jenna said, "Now for another subject that I shall enjoy more than speaking of Ophelia. I heard Rupert calling you Primrose. Do you wish me to use that name as well?"

Her nose wrinkled. "Please continue to address me as Rosie. I do not like the name Primrose."

"Why not? It is lovely."

"I used to think so. Then my aunt told me what Primrose means when one is using the language of flowers to give a secret message to another."

"What does it mean?"

"It means one's heart is not constant in its affections. I prefer Rosie."

"Because that name means love?"

Rosie came to her feet. "Dear me! I never considered that. People may think I am being presumptuous by insisting on being called Rosie."

Jenna laughed. "You are distressing yourself about what is only a silly tradition. Primrose is such a pretty name, and it suits you perfectly with your red hair. I like when I hear Rupert calling you that."

"He uses that name to tease me."

"That is sweet. If . . ." She turned to look at the door behind them.

Before Rosie could do the same, she heard, "Yes, it is sweet, isn't it? Very sweet."

Rosie did not need to see who stood there, because she recognized Ophelia's voice. How long had Ophelia been standing in the doorway listening to their conversation? She knew it could not have been long, because Jenna would have taken note of her eavesdropping before this.

"What do you want, Ophelia?" Jenna asked, not giving Ophelia the courtesy of going to the door to welcome her into the room.

"I had heard you were having a fitting, and I thought I could offer my advice for your wedding gown." She leaned one hand against the door in a pose that showed off her splendid curves and her elegant gown at its best.

"No need. Rosie has helped me already."

"Rosie?" Her laugh was sparkling, but her eyes were not. "Oh, Jenna, how could a country mouse help you with such an important decision? I daresay she has never set foot in a *couturière's* shop. What would she know of fashion?"

"Enough so that I asked *her* opinion."

Ophelia's smile did not dim. "Your choice, Jenna. I hope Henry and your guests agree with Miss Dunsworthy's advice."

"They will. Rosie has excellent taste, I have found."

"Is that so?"

"Yes. She likes what I like, and I am learning she dislikes what I dislike."

"Is that so?"

Rosie flinched when Ophelia's steely eyes focused on her. She could not remain silent any longer and allow Jenna to fight this battle of words alone. But what to say that would not reflect poorly on Jenna and herself as Rupert's guest?

Quietly, she replied, "I do hope others will agree with the advice I offered Jenna."

"Your hopes, Miss Dunsworthy, may not be enough to protect Jenna if she becomes the laughingstock of the Polite World."

"That is unlikely."

Ophelia gave a terse laugh. "I see that you are still limited in your education about the *ton*. I trust Jenna will not be the one who pays for your lack of tuition."

Rosie came to her feet and opened her mouth to snarl back an insult as hideous as the ones Ophelia was speaking. Then she closed it. She would not allow this boorish woman to coerce her into forgetting how one should act. Instead of retorting as she had wished, she said, "I trust that you are correct."

Ophelia stared at her, and, for the first time, Ophelia's smile wavered. When Jenna giggled beside Rosie, Ophelia turned and strode away.

"Oh, dear," Rosie murmured.

"Do not let her arrogance undo your kind ways," Jenna said, setting herself on her feet. "She is accustomed to arguing with every woman she meets. She was quite unprepared to deal with a woman who actually agreed with her."

Rosie nodded, then sighed. She doubted if Ophelia would be unprepared for their next meeting.

# CHAPTER ELEVEN

The early afternoon shower had flushed any warmth from the air, hinting at the cooler days to come. Rosie stepped from the grass and shook one foot, then the other to sweep away the wet clinging to her slippers. She looked down at the basket of flowers she had collected for Jenna's perusal.

The bride-to-be, growing less certain of every decision she had made, had asked several of the female guests at Fortenbury Park to gather their favorite blossoms and bring them to her to consider. Although Rosie believed that the roses and hot house flowers Jenna had already selected were the best choice, she had agreed. She owed Jenna a duty for standing up for her during the uncomfortable discussion with Ophelia.

As she carried the flowers into the house, she bumped into a man who must have just entered the front door. She had not seen him in the shadows within the house.

"Excuse me," she said.

"I should be the one to beg your pardon, miss."

*That* voice was even more familiar than Ophelia's. Blinking to adjust her eyes to the dim light, she looked at hair as dark as Rupert's. This man was not as tall as Rupert, and his broadening waistline suggested he would soon be as round as the Prince Regent.

"Lord Dunsworthy!" Rosie knew she should not be shocked to see her cousin here, but she had not given thought that he would be invited. She should have, because he obviously knew many of the people in the *ton*.

"Cousin . . ." He flushed as brightly as she ever had, warning that he had forgotten her name as he had almost every time they met.

"Primrose Dunsworthy," said Rupert from behind her as he followed her into the house.

"Ah, yes." Her cousin bowed over her hand swiftly. "I should remember. You are Primrose, and you have the red hair. Your aunt—"

"Aunt Millicent is out in the garden with Miss Wallace's mother and several of her aunts." She smiled at Rupert, who seemed to be wavering between a frown and a laugh at her cousin's inability to remember their names. Wanting to tell Rupert that neither she nor Aunt Millicent were bothered by this peculiar habit, for her cousin always had to be reminded of the vicar's name as well, she knew she must not discomfit her cousin further. "They are discussing which flowers would be best for the wedding."

"It is not to be held for another few days." Lord Dunsworthy frowned. "I believe any blossoms they choose now will be dead the time the ceremony begins."

"They are only looking now," Rosie replied. Glancing down at the flowers she held, she added, "These are for Miss Wallace to consider in her room, because she is too busy to visit the garden herself. As you may guess, she is as eager as Mr. Jordan to have everything perfect for the ceremony and the wedding breakfast."

Lord Dunsworthy handed his hat to a footman. "While we are on this subject, I suppose I should offer an invitation to you and your aunt before I forget."

"An invitation to what?"

"My own nuptials."

"Congratulations, Dunsworthy." Rupert smiled broadly. "I had not heard that you had become betrothed."

"Really? I thought Lydia had informed everyone on the island by now."

"Lydia? Lydia Vokey?"

He nodded. "Do you know her?"

"I cannot say I have had the honor of being introduced to her, but we do have mutual acquaintances who have spoken of her."

When Rupert added nothing more, Rosie said, "Let us know the date you have set, and Aunt Millicent and I will be delighted to come to the wedding."

He nodded and started to walk away, then added, "Do let Wandersee know of the wedding and that he and his wife are most welcome, will you?"

"Yes." She refused to let her hands clench into fists. She could put up with his inability to recall her name or anyone else's in Dunstanbury because he did not consider them of enough importance, but this was an insult of the first order. Her cousin had invited her and Aunt Millicent only as a way to persuade Lucian to attend. Bother! Her cousin was not worthy of the title of Lord Dunsworthy, but nothing could change that.

Rupert said nothing as Lord Dunsworthy followed a footman up the stairs to whatever chamber had been set aside for his use. She appreciated the fact that Rupert did not pepper her with questions about her cousin.

Setting her basket on a nearby table, she untied her bonnet. A servant appeared instantly, and Rosie asked, "Will you please have these flowers taken to Miss Wallace's room right away?"

"Yes, miss." The maid picked up the basket and hurried up the stairs.

Rupert laughed. "More flowers for Jenna to choose from? It might be simpler just to cut every blossom in the garden and crowd them into the chapel."

"I doubt if anything could be deemed simpler now." She glanced toward the stairs, then wished she had not, for when she looked back at Rupert, his smile was gone.

"Your cousin makes you uncomfortable, doesn't he?"

"Yes, because he reminds me that my brother is dead." Her smile was sad. "Not that I shall ever forget Kevin's death, you must understand."

"I do understand."

"Thank you." She picked up a leaf that had fallen from her basket and twirled it around her fingers. "It is only in the last few months that my sister has been willing to speak of him."

"It is not easy to lose someone unexpectedly."

"You speak as if you know."

"I do."

He was silent for so long that Rosie had to fight not to blurt out the questions that exploded through her head. His smile returned, sad, as he said, "Forgive me, Rosie, for forcing my dismals upon you. It has been barely more than a year since my father died."

"It was unexpected?"

"He was thrown from his horse during a hunt at a friend's dirty acres. He had so recently inherited the family's title from his late brother that many people talk about the title coming directly from my uncle to me."

"Oh, I am so sorry." She hesitated, then said, "Rupert, I know those are banal words, but I do mean them. I would never have wished a lingering illness upon my brother. Yet, I was unprepared for his loss."

"Your words are perfect." He offered his arm. When she put her hand on it, he said, "I believe I know the very thing to put a smile back on our faces."

"Introducing me to my cousin's betrothed?"

He laughed. "No, for she will not be attending the wedding this weekend. However, I can assure you that such a meeting would be certain to put a smile on your face. Lydia Vokey has a reputation for having a sharp tongue, and I fear your cousin is due to endure many curtain-lectures during his married life."

Rosie tried to hold back her own laugh but could not. "I must try to have more sympathy for my cousin in the future."

"He is making his own bed, if you will excuse the description." He led her back out of the house. As she tied her bonnet back beneath her chin again, they walked down the steps toward the water garden.

"Such a description is not inappropriate." She hesitated as she gazed at the building beside the wide pool that appeared to be much deeper than the one at Dunsworthy Hall. The building was made of wood and stone, and it had a single window. Wide doors were closed, but she guessed small boats waited behind them for someone to decide to enjoy a row across the pond. When she looked back at Rupert, she asked, "Is Miss Vokey really so bad?"

"No. It *is* a good match because her son will inherit a title, and her father's money will fund the renovations of Dunsworthy Hall that your cousin has been lamenting he has been unable to do for the past year."

"I guess the rainbow was right after all. My cousin has found a pot of gold."

"What rainbow?"

"The one I saw arching toward Dunsworthy Hall on the day you arrived in Dunstanbury."

"Ah, I recall the pretty sight." He flashed her a smile. "One of several pretty sights I encountered upon entering Dunstanbury."

"Rupert, please do not say such things to me." She stared at the boathouse again, but this time sightlessly. How ironic that she should chide him when his words pleased her so! But she could create nothing but melancholy by listening to her heart, which teased her to flirt with him as boldly as Ophelia had.

"I was trying to compliment you."

She paused and faced him. Although she longed to shout that she did not want him to act toward her as if she were the same as Ophelia, she held back those words. Rather she said, "I appreciate that, but I liked when you treated me with camaraderie while we spoke of what we had read."

"You are a continuous surprise."

"Because I wish to be offered your respect rather than being lathered with nothing-sayings?"

"Why can't I offer you both respect and admiration?"

Rosie fought not to, but she laughed. "There is no answer I can give to that question."

"Then mayhap you can give me an answer to *this* question."

"I shall try."

"Did you see where the other end of the rainbow was?"

Startled that he was still talking about that, she said, "No."

"It dropped very close to where your cottage is."

This time, she did not try to restrain her laugh. "I shall have to look for that pot of gold when I return to Dunsworthy Dower Cottage."

"There are those, such as me, who say the treasure has already been discovered." He raised his hand when she was about to give him a back-answer. "I am not lauding you, Rosie. I speak instead of your strawberry tart. You have no idea how many times I have thought about enjoying that sweet again."

"I would gladly share the receipt with your kitchen."

"But then I would have to find something else to fantasize about."

She drew away when his words seemed to be taking a turn that was far too intimate again. In dismay, she realized they were out of sight from the house. Then she relaxed. He had always been a gentleman. As well, someone looking from the uppermost floor would be able to see them in this garden, so they were not acting out of hand to be here.

Sitting on a bench that was edged by bushes that no longer were flowering, Rosie said, "I hope you have other things to dream about."

"I do have other dreams."

"Dreams of discovering the key to the hiero-glyphics."

"That is one." He sat beside her and kicked a pebble into the pond. "Mayhap I shall someday. Assuming we all survive Henry and Jenna's wedding."

"That is a large assumption now."

"And you, Rosie? What dreams do you have?" He chuckled. "If I were to guess, I would wager that it had to do with music. Your aunt tells me that you used to write down your melodies."

"She knows about that?"

"Your aunt does not miss much of what is happening around her."

"Something that Kevin and Bianca used to bemoan."

"Do you still write down your melodies?"

She nodded. "I have been working on the song you heard."

"I hope you will share the whole of it with me when it is done."

"First, I must finish it."

He smiled at her. "You did not answer me, Rosie. Where do your dreams take you?"

"I used to imagine being in the music room of the Prince Regent's glorious house in Brighton. I have heard that there is an incredible pipe organ there."

"And you would sing a song of your own writing?"

"Yes." She gazed up at the sky where clouds were slipping along an invisible path. "I would entertain the Prince Regent and his guests with a score that would set their hearts to beating with excitement and sorrow and endless hope. When I was done, they would applaud, and I would take my bow before joining them for tea and a discussion of the newest music by great composers."

"You must have dreamed that often to have so many details."

"Probably no more times than you have dreamed of traveling along the Nile."

He leaned his elbow on the back of the seat and rested his chin on his palm as he gazed at her. "Is performing for the Prince Regent the only dream you have, Rosie?"

She wanted to tell him that the rest of her dreams were too private to share, but her voice withered away as she stared into his eyes. A gentle compassion brightened them along with something else. She was not sure what that something else was. It teased her to find out, to dare to delve past the obvious to discover the truth kept hidden by this closely restrained man.

"I have other dreams," she heard herself saying before she could halt herself.

"What are they?"

"A dream of traveling to London and seeing the grandeur that I have read about." She smiled. "I also have a dream of having a library that is ever-changing, so that when I have read one book another appears for me to devour."

"And do you think you shall ever possess such a library?"

"Maybe. Someday maybe, but dreams do not always need to come true, although I have to own that the best ones should." What was it about his honest eyes that was mesmerizing? And his smile . . . His endearing expression could send even a cautious woman into a tizzy within seconds.

"And I wager that you are waiting for your knight in shining armor, too."

Whether it was the hint of sarcasm in his voice or his choice of words, she looked away. She was an air-dreamer! She should know better. Rupert had given her no more than an engaging grin and she was ready to spill her heart's most precious secrets to him.

Letting irritation sift into her voice, she fired back, "I assure you, Rupert, that I do not need to be rescued from my quiet life by some knight on his charger. A woman who wishes to make grand dreams like mine come true must learn to depend on herself."

"That is a novel opinion."

"It is the one I have learned from Aunt Millicent."

"She certainly is proof of what she says. She has taught you to be independent."

"You make it sound like an intolerable state."

"Quite to the contrary," he said with another smile. "If I may be completely honest, I must say that I admire how both you and your aunt have made an extraordinary life for yourself beyond the realm of the Polite World."

"In spite of what the *ton* seems to believe, the apparently impolite world has many wonders that cannot be seen from within the narrow confines of the social whirl of the Season."

His smile warmed. "You are right yet again, Rosie. It is a pleasure to have a chance to talk with someone who speaks her mind instead of trying to say what it is assumed I wish to hear."

"If I were to do that, it would be just as easy for you to speak to your reflection in a glass."

"Easy, mayhap. Pleasurable, no." His hand rose toward her cheek, then drew back.

She held her breath, unsure, as she had been when he had touched her in the sitting room at the cottage. He murmured something. It might have been her name or a question, but she could not hear it past her frantic heartbeat. Again his hand reached out to her. Gently, as if she were as fragile as one of the clouds floating overhead, he caressed the curve of her face.

Closing her eyes, she sank into the rapture of the light brush of his fingertips against her cheek. A quiver shot through her, and she opened her eyes to see pleasure in his. She could not tell if he was as startled as she was by this delight. Then, as his fingers outlined the shape of her cheekbone, she knew that this was far more than just the friendship she had asked for. If he had never touched her, even this chastely, she might have been able to deny that she wanted much more. Now it was impossible.

Staring up into his eyes, which revealed his longing to touch more than her face, she told herself to slide away and stand and leave before the situation could become even more complicated. But she wanted to stay in this fantasy. She wanted to stay in this fantasy with him.

His fingers under her chin brought her lips toward his. Every inch of her waited for the sensation of his mouth on hers. She could not guess what it would be like, but she knew it would not be the same as when Constable Powers had kissed her. This kiss she wanted.

Rosie froze at the sound of laughter from the direction of the pond. She pulled away and stared at Rupert in disbelief. Had every bit of good sense fled when he touched her? Yes, and that thought unnerved her.

"Rosie, I—"

"Please do not say anything," she whispered. "If you apologize, it will make me feel even worse."

"I was not going to apologize." He waved to his brother, who called to him, and Jenna. Looking back at Rosie, he regarded her with an intensity she had never seen before. "I could never be so dishonest with you. It would be a lie to suggest I was not acting upon an impulse that has been haunting me since I saw you in Dunstanbury."

She stared at her clasped fingers because meeting his eyes was too difficult when she could not be as honest as she wished. "I fear the discussion of dreams and possibilities that should stay only dreams led us astray."

"Astray? Is that what you think?" He put his crooked finger under her chin and brought her face up toward his again.

"Don't, Rupert," she whispered. "Please don't."

Rupert nodded as he reluctantly drew his finger away from Rosie's soft skin. He did not want to own that she was correct. He had overstepped the boundaries of decent behavior by leading her into this discussion in such a secluded place and then letting his own desires take control of him.

But how was it possible to be with this so very desirable woman and keep one's head about oneself? He had no answer for that question. Yet he must have one, because he could not chance distressing her more, nor could he chance compromising her in any manner. Then she would avoid him as surely as he tried to avoid Ophelia, who *wanted* him to compromise her.

By thunder! The answer was simple.

Forcing a smile as he glanced over his shoulder to discover Henry and Jenna had paused by a flowering shrub, he said, "Rosie, I have been remiss as your host."

"Remiss?" Confusion filled her green eyes.

"I offered you books to read and discussed the contents with you, but I have yet to show you the fragments I have in my office."

"The fragments of Egyptian writing?"

"Yes." He could not help being pleased by her eager response, although he wished it had been to his kiss. *Forget that! She has made her opinions on that matter quite clear.* "I would be grateful if you would look at them and give me your opinion."

"My opinion?" She laughed, the joy returning to her voice. "I am afraid my opinion is very untutored."

"Nevertheless, I would be grateful to have your opinion."

"On what?" asked his brother as he and Jenna drew even with the bench.

Rupert came to his feet and hoped his smile hid his annoyance that Henry's voice had intruded on his chance to taste Rosie's lips. Clapping his brother on the shoulder, he said, "Nothing that would interest you, Henry. We are speaking of the Egyptian artifacts, not the plans for your wedding."

"Do not even speak of that." Henry rolled his eyes. "If my beloved Jenna asks one more time which flowers I would like for the tables for the wedding breakfast, I fear I shall run off and join Napoleon in his exile. The next thing you know, she shall be pestering me about the style of her gown."

"Henry," Jenna returned, "*that* is an aspect of the

wedding you do not need to fret about. Rosie has kindly given me her opinions, which I trust on that subject far more than I do yours, my dear." She smiled as she kissed him on the cheek. "I assure you that I will not shame you when I meet you in front of the vicar."

He blushed red. "My beloved Jenna, I never would have suggested otherwise. Rosie, Rupert, you must not think—"

"Neither of them does!" Jenna squeezed his hand. "I am hoaxing you."

His color began to return to its customary shade, and Rupert chuckled.

"Henry, you are worrying far too much," Rupert said.

"I wish our wedding to be perfect." Again he looked at Rosie. "You understand, don't you?"

Rosie hesitated, and Rupert laughed again. "Henry, you are putting our guest in a difficult position. If she agrees with Jenna that you are agonizing too much over the ceremony and the gathering, you may take insult. If she is not honest, she will never forgive herself when you swoon at the altar because one of the posies is tilted the wrong way."

"I did not wish your comments, Rupert. I asked Rosie. What do *you* think?" he asked impatiently.

"I understand that you wish to have the wedding be perfect just as you wish the rest of your lives together to be perfect," Rosie replied.

Both Jenna and Henry smiled, but Rupert heard Rosie's breath flow out of her in a sigh so soft neither of the others noticed it. A sigh of relief? He did not blame her, for his brother had been rude to put such a question to her. He took her hand and drew her to her feet.

"Now that you have finished bothering Rosie with your ludicrous questions," Rupert said, "we will leave you to whatever tasks you have before the wedding."

As he had hoped, that comment started Jenna and his brother discussing matters of flowers and their guests. He shook his head as he led Rosie back to the house.

"Do not be judgmental," she said, surprising him, for there was no humor behind her scold.

"Don't you agree that they are being silly to worry about every detail of this wedding as if no one ever married before this?"

"Yes, I do, but they are enjoying themselves immensely by agonizing over every tiny detail. Do not deny them that pleasure."

Although he wanted to demand how she could ask that of him when she had denied herself and him *their* pleasure, he nodded. Then he realized she was not looking at him. Her gaze was focused on the pond, and he guessed her thoughts were even more distant. Or were they turned within as she thought of what they almost had shared?

"Just promise me one thing, my dear Primrose," he said quietly.

"Rupert! How many times must I ask you not to address me with that name?"

"I wanted to be sure you were listening to me when you were looking so moonily across the garden."

"I am listening. Now."

"Good. So promise me that if I am ever so foolish over love, you will set me to rights speedily."

"I promise you that." She smiled at him. "If you do the same for me."

"Agreed." He took her hand in his. Although he

had meant to shake it, he lifted it and pressed it to his cheek.

Delight flared in her eyes, then she pulled her hand away. She mumbled some excuse to him. He did not need to understand the words, for he perceived their meaning as, with a flurry of her skirts, she hurried back toward the house as if he were giving chase.

He did not. He followed more slowly, knowing that she was already trying to keep the promise she had just made him. She would prevent him from letting love persuade him to something stupid . . . especially with her.

# CHAPTER TWELVE

Playing with fire was stupid.

Rosie knew that, but, even so, she could not resist Rupert's invitation to examine the fragments that had come from Egypt. Her attempt to get Aunt Millicent's opinion first had been futile, because her aunt had joined Mrs. Wallace for luncheon. Even if she had had the chance to discuss her uncertainty with her aunt, the only advice she would have received would be to do what Rosie deemed right.

Was it wise to meet Rupert in his book-room after she had almost melted at his touch? She could not guess, but she was on her way to his book-room. Simply to see the fragments, or was it in hopes of more?

When she reached his book-room, the door was wide open. Rupert must realize the danger of them being alone, too. Relieved that she would not have to worry about letting her senses overmaster her—again—she entered the room with its overcrowded bookshelves and stacks of books on the floor and windowsills. She slowly turned, viewing the room from every angle. *This* was exactly what she had envisioned for her imaginary library.

"How wonderful!" she whispered.

"I am afraid there are a finite number of books, not an endlessly changing collection." Rupert put down what looked like a small, pale brown stone, but she knew it was one of the fragments.

She waited for the pulse of excitement that she had expected when she finally saw the artifacts he had here at Fortenbury Park. It did not come. Instead of staring at the fragments, she could not pull her gaze from Rupert. She paused in mid-step as the expression in his dark eyes warned her that he was finding it impossible to forget what had happened in the water garden.

Just as she was.

Rosie stepped backward as he moved toward her. When he leaned one hand negligently against the bookcase and smiled, she wondered why she was acting guilty about something that had not happened. They had not kissed. Wanting to kiss him could not be wrong as long as she kept it only a fantasy. They could act as if everything remained the same while they studied the fragments together . . . couldn't they?

"Are there other books on the discoveries in Egypt?" she asked when she had found her voice again.

"This whole shelf." He patted the one he had been leaning against. "You are welcome to read any that you wish. Then we can discuss what you have read instead of which flowers belong on the wedding breakfast tables and which ones should be showcased in the chapel."

Rosie told herself that she should not be amazed that he had his books in such precise order. "You are intimidating, you know," she said, smiling.

"Me?" He seemed honestly astonished.

"Yes, you. You have intimidated most of your guests by speaking eloquently of your studies."

"But I have not intimidated you at all."

"No . . ." She laughed. "Mayhap a bit."

"You have no reason to be unnerved by me and my comments about what I have studied."

"I do not refer to those comments, but to the ones you have made to your brother and Jenna."

"I have an idea that much of what I said you would like to say."

"Mayhap a bit," she said as she had before. Sitting on a chair in front of the closer window, she watched as he drew up another chair close to hers.

Rupert laughed as he sat and relaxed back against his chair. "By thunder, Rosie! I say again what I have said many times."

"And what is that?"

"That you are a most uncommon woman."

"Is that so?"

"Do not take offense at what is meant to be a compliment."

"I collect it would be far worse if you considered me a most common woman."

"Eureka!"

Rosie stared at him, startled by his outburst. When she heard footfalls pause in the corridor, she knew the sound of his voice had reached ears beyond her own.

"Eureka?" she asked. "You sound as if you have made a great discovery, but you have confused me utterly."

"No, your comment confirmed what I had already guessed."

"That I am not a common woman?"

He laughed again. "That I already knew. What

you confirmed is the fact that you have a skill with words few others can claim."

"A skill that is necessary for survival in the Dunsworthy family."

"Then I see you have no worry about not surviving." He rested his arm on his knees and leaned toward her. "So why are you quiet when others are about?"

"Whetted words must be sheathed before they hurt someone."

"Only when they speak the truth."

"Which I am afraid I find myself compelled to do at the very most inopportune times." She tried to smile but failed miserably.

"So you remain silent."

"Yes."

"A shame."

"Mayhap, but it is the way I am."

He took her hands between his and gave them a quick squeeze before she could yank them back. He released them as swiftly as he had grasped them. Coming to his feet, he held out his hand as he said, "I believe you have waited long enough."

She stared up at him, unable to look beyond his lips. As they formed each word, she feared he would hear the swift thunder of her heart. Aunt Millicent's voice warning her always to think carefully when with a man came back to taunt her.

"I have?" she whispered.

"Yes, I believe you have." He lifted a strand off her shoulder and rubbed it between his fingers with slow, smooth strokes. "One should not have to wait forever to allow a dream to come true."

She was completely unable to speak as she looked up at him. So many thoughts danced through her head, but only one remained. The dream of stepping into his arms as he kissed her. Was she deranged? Why was she allowing a single mistake—a mistake that was not even her own—to beguile her into making an even greater one?

"Why are you hesitating?" he asked. "Don't you want to see the tablets?"

Rosie shook her silly thoughts from her mind and nodded. How many more ways could she prove to herself—but hopefully not to him—that she was want-witted? He had been speaking only of looking at the tablets.

As she put her hand on his and let him draw her to her feet, the quiver she had thought would surge through her when she saw the fragments came now when his fingers closed over hers. When he led her to the desk where he kept his valuable artifacts, she was glad he kept his gaze on them and not on her. She did not want him to see how his very touch undid her.

He picked up one of the fragments and placed it in her hand. Smiling, he said, "This one is much finer than the samples you saw at Jordan Court where my brother keeps some only as conversation pieces."

Rosie turned the stone over and saw the deeply carved images of people and birds and other items that seemed to have no pattern. "Oh, my," she whispered.

"'Oh, my'?"

"Why are you repeating back my words to me?"

He smiled. "I am enjoying your pleasure with your first sight of these tablets. It reminds me of my own when I unwrapped them."

"It is beyond amazing." She ran her finger along the tablet, letting her skin explore each indentation in the stone. "I try to think of how many millennia ago these symbols were carved, and I am over-awed. Did the person who engraved this stone ever imagine that we would be touching it so many centuries later?"

"His thoughts were probably on the concerns of his life. His family, his job, what would happen if the Nile flooded before he was finished with the task of completing whatever this is meant to say."

She laughed as she cradled the stone in her hand. "You make these incredible fragments seem prosaic."

"They were to the people who made them." He touched one of the symbols. "Mayhap they were chiseling these with a listing of the events of their commonplace lives or what they planned to have for dinner that evening."

"But no one knows that for certain."

"It is something anyone who makes an attempt to read them must keep in mind. I own that I would be vastly disappointed if they contain only a shopping list."

"I will have a difficult time viewing them as ancient newspapers."

"But that is what many of them are." He smiled as he took the fragment and placed it with care next to the others. "I am telling you what you *should* think—and what I *should* think, although I own it is difficult to consider these commonplace. After almost five years of study, I own to a pulse of awe each time I look at them."

"Five years?"

"It is a long time to be fascinated with something old and dusty." He chuckled. "That is what Henry is fond of telling me."

"He believes it is boring . . . as Ophelia does."

"So you have noticed that?"

"How could I fail to notice how she becomes vexed any time the subject turns to these?"

He drew a book off a shelf behind him. When he put it on the desk, it fell open to a page. He pointed out the drawing in the book and then one of the fragments. As she compared the two and listened to his insights on them, she wondered if she had ever been happier. She did not want this moment to end.

Ever.


"Aunt Millicent, I do not think I have ever been so intrigued by anything in my whole life." Rosie walked with her aunt through the morning sunshine. "Touching something so old is incredible."

"I am glad you are enjoying yourself here." She smiled as they emerged onto the avenue and started back toward the house.

"Did you think I would not?"

"I thought some . . . How shall I put this nicely? I thought some of Rupert's guests would be troublesome to you."

"If you are speaking of Ophelia King, you need not worry. She has not spoken a word to me since we last spoke in Jenna's rooms."

"Do not become complacent and believe that situation will continue."

Rosie stopped and stared at her aunt. "You make it sound as if there is a war going on."

"Ophelia believes there is. A war to win the title of Lady Rupert Fortenbury."

"It is a war she is fighting alone. Rupert and I know it is best to remain only friends."

"Only?"

Wishing she had thought before she had spoken, Rosie hurried to answer. "Do not jump upon each word I say, Aunt Millicent, as if it held a secret meaning. I am enjoying studying the artifacts with Rupert."

"Nothing more?"

"No." She was not being false with her aunt. Not completely false, she amended silently. Both she and Rupert had taken care while examining the artifacts to keep their conversation focused on the stones and not on how each inadvertent touch was as riveting as lightning slicing through a tree.

"I am sorry to hear that," Aunt Millicent said.

"Really?"

"Yes, really." She continued along the broad road between the sentinel trees. "Forgive me for speaking like a matchmaker, Rosie, but even a witless fool could see that you and Rupert relish each other's company with an unusual zest."

"We share a common interest."

"Which is more than many do who fall in love." Aunt Millicent shrugged, then resettled her crocheted shawl around her shoulders. "Mayhap you are wise to stay out of the battle that Miss King is eager to engage you in."

"The only one Ophelia is eager to be engaged with is Rupert." Her laugh fell flat, and she wished she had kept it from bursting forth.

Aunt Millicent put her arm around Rosie and smiled. "I know what you mean. Do not fret. Enjoy this peek at the *ton* and their ways. Soon we will be returning to Dunstanbury and our own ways."

"Yes." Rosie added nothing else as Aunt Millicent began to talk about the harvest festival that was always held at the beginning of October. Each year, Rosie had anticipated its arrival eagerly. Now it was only something that would happen after she bid Rupert farewell. She did not doubt that he would call on occasion at Dunsworthy Dower Cottage to bring her a book or to get some of her strawberry tart. That would be slim comfort when she had become accustomed to seeing him every day at Fortenbury Park.

Going into the house and up the stairs with her aunt, she wished she could think of an excuse to bow out of joining her aunt in the lovely rooms Aunt Millicent was using. Rupert had selected the perfect room for Aunt Millicent. The biggest window offered a view of the avenue and the flower clock that was set behind a hedge beyond the front door.

Her aunt set her bonnet on a japan table by the doorway and went to that window. "Rosie, do not let me forget to speak with Rupert's head gardener before we leave. I hope to persuade him to give me his secret to how he grows such lush roses."

"I offered to give the kitchen my receipt for my strawberry tart." She smiled, genuinely this time. "Mayhap we can work an exchange."

"An excellent idea. The roses in the . . ." She stared out the window, then motioned wildly. "Rosie, do you recognize that man?"

"Which one?" she asked, going to the window. On the avenue below, several men were gathered around a sleek carriage she had not seen before.

"The one stepping out of the phaeton. He looks so familiar. If we saw him at Henry's house, we . . ."

Rosie turned when her aunt's voice trailed off again. Aunt Millicent's face was becoming the color of the gray clouds gathering on the western horizon.

Taking Aunt Millicent by the arm, Rosie steered her to a chair.

"Are you ill?" she asked, concerned, for this behavior was out of the ordinary for her aunt.

"Ill?"

Rosie chafed her aunt's left wrist, then her right. Aunt Millicent's hands were icy, and her gaze seemed focused on the opposite wall.

"What is wrong?" asked Rosie.

"That man—"

"You recognize him?"

"Yes." Aunt Millicent turned to her. "Rosie, my dear child, you must do me a great favor."

"You know I would gladly do anything for you." She smiled. "Save have tea with Ophelia."

At the jest, Aunt Millicent's face eased from its tense lines but remained somber. "I will endeavor to remember that."

"Tell me what you wish me to do."

"If you see that man approaching me, please intrude with an excuse that requires me to leave immediately."

"Why? Who is he?"

"Quinn . . . Sir Alexander Quinley." She rubbed her hands together as she came to her feet. "The man I once had hoped to wed."

Rosie glanced toward the window, wanting to catch a better view of the man who had touched her aunt's heart. "But that is grand, Aunt Millicent! I am sure that any differences that prevented your wedding are in the past, so why not take this opportunity to heal those old wounds?"

"I do not want to heal them." Aunt Millicent walked out of the sitting room and into her bedchamber. The door shut resoundingly behind her.

Before Rosie could take a single step, she heard the key turn in her aunt's door. What had happened that her aunt could not put aside so many years later?

Rosie went to the window, drawing back the drapes and the sheer curtains beneath them. The man pointed out by her aunt was now talking to Henry, so she took the opportunity to appraise him.

Sir Alexander Quinley was not as tall as Henry, but he carried himself with obvious pride. He had black hair sprinkled with gray exactly like the horse drawing his carriage. When he tilted his head back in laughter, she saw he also had the most remarkable mustache she had ever seen. It was thick and covered both lips.

This man had hurt her aunt deeply, and Rosie was determined to find out why. Leaving her bonnet and shawl in her aunt's room, she hurried to where she could watch Sir Alexander enter the house. Mayhap some motion or comment would give her the clue she needed. She edged along the gallery railing until she could get a good view of the entry below.

"Peeking through the railing is a task best left to children." Rupert's laugh followed his words.

When she turned to see him looking breathtakingly handsome in leather riding breeches and a shirt that was open at the collar, she wondered if she could draw in enough air to answer. He was carrying his coat folded over his arm, and he draped it atop the railing as he came to stand beside her.

"Whom are you spying on?" he asked.

"What makes you think I am spying?"

"You jumped so high when I spoke that I feared you would dash your head against the ceiling."

"You are exaggerating."

He laughed again. "Not much. Please answer my question. Whom are you spying on?"

"Him." She pointed gracelessly to Sir Alexander.

"Sir Alexander Quinley? I did not know that you even knew the man."

"I don't, but Aunt Millicent does."

"Why are *you* spying on him? Where is Millicent?"

"Resting," she replied.

Rupert nodded, but Rosie doubted if he believed her half-truth. He took her arm and led her to a padded bench away from the railing. Sitting beside her, he said, "You do not tell out-and-outers well, Rosie."

"I know."

"Will you tell me the truth?"

She rubbed her abruptly cold hands together. "I should not be speaking of my aunt and her past."

"Do you think I will rush from here to repeat into every ear what you tell me?"

"No."

"Then tell me what is wrong. Your words will go no further than my ears."

Rosie smiled. She could trust him, and that was a wonderful feeling. She could not recall the last time she had been able to trust anyone outside her family.

In addition, Rupert was insightful. Even in the midst of the upheaval preceding his brother's wedding, he was certain to notice a change in Aunt Millicent the first time he encountered her. After all, Aunt Millicent had not sworn her to silence. Mayhap Aunt Millicent did not believe she must ask for such a vow, because she knew that Rosie was not a prattler.

Yet, Rupert might know of a way to ease Aunt

Millicent's despair. Quinn must be a friend of the Jordan family if he was here for the wedding.

"You are right. I am concerned about Aunt Millicent," she said quietly.

"She has not taken ill, has she?"

"Not as you mean."

"What do *you* mean?"

Rosie stood and went to put her hand on the railing again. "She is sick at heart."

"At heart? Has someone spoken cruelly to her?"

"No."

As she related what little she knew, he nodded. "I did hear whispers of some sort of scandal when your aunt first arrived at Jordan Court with you and your sister and Wandersee."

"Scandal?" Her eyes widened. "Aunt Millicent? They must be mistaken."

"Having come to know your aunt, I agree. However, her actions suggest something bad happened."

"She fell in love with him and the love was not returned is what I guess happened." She sighed. "Now she wants to avoid him. I am afraid I do not understand love."

"Who does?"

"The Egyptians did." She smiled reluctantly. "You can see that in the way that the pictures of both men and women are carved together on their great structures. A pharaoh must have loved his wife to have her picture there."

"But from the figures carved into the tombs, a pharaoh is also believed to have had concubines and slaves in what we now would call a seraglio. In addition, it appears most pharaohs had more than one wife."

She shook her head. "From what I have seen since we arrived at Fortenbury Park, making a single match is a very complicated affair. To make multiple ones . . . I shudder at the very idea."

"But you are thinking like a woman of this time instead of as the pharaoh and his court thought. First of all, most marriages were political. He would wed his sister to guarantee that the blood of his son was undiluted. Other wives as well as concubines joined his household through the efforts of his ministers, who were trying to keep the peace and make alliances."

"Not a wonderful alternative, but . . ."

His fingers against her cheek tipped her face up gently. When she stepped away from him again, he asked, "What else is wrong, Rosie?"

She could not be as forthright with him about the state of her own heart, so she replied, "I can think only of my aunt at the moment. Other matters must be pushed aside."

"I shall speak with Quinn, if you wish."

Facing him, she was not surprised to discover him only an arm's length from her. His insatiable curiosity would not let him sit still. Her ambiguous words had presented him with a puzzle he would want to unravel, as he did the meaning of the hieroglyphics.

"No." She smiled. "There is no need to look as if you are about to ask some gentleman to name his friends and arrange for you to meet him on the dueling green."

"*I* look like that? Me?"

"Yes."

"Amazing." He looked past her. "I believe you are

right, but I would like to see this incredible expression for myself."

Hoping that she could keep the conversation going in this direction and away from her aunt, Rosie said, "There is a glass just down the corridor." She moved to walk past him. "If—"

He put out his arm to block her way. He did not touch her, but she had to fight her feet, which teased her to take another step forward as her hand drew his arm around her. Had her face revealed the truth? It must have, because his arm slowly lowered to his side. Before she could continue past him, his other hand rose to cup her shoulder.

"Rosie," he whispered as if he feared one of the portraits along the gallery would overhear, "something else is bothering you deeply. I know we have not known each other long, but I had hoped that you had become well enough acquainted with me to realize that my offer to help you is sincere."

"I do believe it is, but I cannot think of anything but my aunt now."

"You find a sanctuary from your own emotions in someone else's, don't you?"

"How can you say something like that?"

"Because I do the same." He picked up his coat from the railing. "If you wish to talk with me, Rosie, you know where to find me."

She *did* know where to find him. He would be with the fragments and books that allowed him to flee the world when he wanted to hide his own thoughts. But those fragments and books had failed him, for his thoughts had been so very clear on his face when he touched her.

He wanted to continue what his brother and Jenna had interrupted in the water garden. And so did she, but she had seen what the longing for a man's kisses and touch had done to her aunt. Instead of being her customary cheerful self, Aunt Millicent was a gray wraith who hid in her private chambers, unwilling to see anyone because that chanced meeting the man who had stolen her heart and then dashed it to pieces.

Would Rupert do the same to her? She could not imagine him intentionally hurting her, but she had seen that he was intent on keeping the quiet, studious life he had now. Yes, he might be willing to steal a few kisses—and anything else she allowed. Yet, he clearly thought his brother was silly to be embarking upon marriage.

She would be wise to learn from her aunt's mistakes before she repeated them. She hoped she still could, for her heart was teasing her not to listen to caution.

# CHAPTER THIRTEEN

"You wish to know what I think? I think that you are an addle-pate to believe your bulky carriage can best my swift phaeton." Sir Alexander put his cup of coffee back on the table and looked along it to where Henry was grinning.

Rosie heard Jenna's giggle and took a sip of her tea. She had been watching Sir Alexander all during breakfast, but she could find no fault with him. He was kindhearted and witty and obviously respected by the other guests. Even though Ophelia was sitting between him and Mr. Byrne, Sir Alexander seemed indifferent to her flirtations. That endeared him instantly to Rosie, and again the questions of what had happened between him and her aunt plagued her.

Henry took a bite of his roll, then used it to emphasize his point as he leaned toward Sir Alexander. "I was not speaking of my carriage, Quinn. It is not a racing vehicle. I was speaking of my uncle's."

"Byrne's carriage?" Sir Alexander waved his hand with disdain before turning to look past Ophelia to Rupert's uncle. "I have seen your fusty vehicle, Byrne. It will be left behind my phaeton in a cloud of dust before we have gone a mile."

"Do you honestly believe that?" Mr. Byrne grinned.

"I would not have said so if I did not."

"Would you be willing to wager on that?" asked Henry, and the two men glanced at each other and grinned broadly.

"A capital idea!" Mr. Byrne crowed.

"Just the way to prove to Byrne that he was a beef-head to speak so of his carriage," seconded Sir Alexander.

Rosie listened to the men debating how much should be wagered and where the race should be run, but she watched Ophelia. The brunette could not hide her dismay that the men were talking around her instead of keeping her as the center of attention.

"You are grinning way too widely," Jenna whispered as she leaned toward Rosie. "If she sees you, she will do whatever she can to make your life even more miserable."

"She will not see me." Rosie picked up her cup and sipped again, knowing that the action hid her expression.

"Or me." Jenna turned to rest her chin on her palm in a pose that suggested she was gazing at her betrothed with utter devotion. Still, Rosie could see her lips twitching.

In quick order, Mr. Byrne and Sir Alexander had set the parameters of the race as well as a wager of 100 pounds. Rosie told herself not to be shocked by such an amount of money being bet on a single race of just three miles. Betting such high amounts was another of the ways of the *ton* that were foreign to her. The men excused themselves to get their carriages ready, laughing in anticipation of the race to come. From watching them, she would have guessed they had come to Fortenbury Park solely for the race, for all talk of the wedding had been shunted aside.

Henry stood and held out his hand to Jenna. "Shall we watch the race, sweetheart? I want to be certain my side wager on Quinn is won."

"What a wondrous idea!"

Rosie was amazed that Jenna could be excited about a carriage race. She doubted if she would ever understand the odd ways of the *ton.*

"I knew it would not take long for them to set their minds on a contest," Rupert said as he entered the breakfast-parlor. His dark coat was the perfect contrast to the pale green walls. With a laugh, he added, "I saw Uncle Victor had his eye on Quinn's carriage as soon as it arrived yesterday. Would you like to watch the race, too?"

Ophelia jumped up and slipped her arm through his. "Of course I would, my dearest Rupert."

He disengaged his arm from her as he continued to smile. "Uncle Victor said he was depending on you to ride with him to be his good luck charm."

"In his carriage?"

"That is what he told me."

"How exciting to be part of the race!" Ophelia kissed him on the cheek, gave the others another of her superior smiles, and rushed out of the room.

"Well done," Henry crowed as he cuffed his brother's shoulder and laughed. "Uncle Victor is going to be thrilled to have her with him, and you have pried her covetous hand off you."

"Henry, your poor manners in speaking of Ophelia make you sound as if you have been giving a bottle a black eye."

"At this hour?" He smiled at Jenna. "Mayhap it is because I am intoxicated with my beloved's smile."

Rosie laughed when Jenna did, but her laughter faltered when Rupert turned to her and asked, "Would you like to ride with me to watch the end of the race?"

"Yes, but Aunt Millicent—"

"Is welcome to join us as well."

"Let me find her and get my bonnet."

He smiled. "Not your best one. This race shall be dusty."

She did not answer. She had only one bonnet, but fortunately it was a straw one that would brush clean readily. Hurrying up the stairs at a most unladylike speed, she rushed into her room. She paused only long enough to put the sheet with the words for her song back into the drawer where she kept it when she was not trying to make the words come together in tempo with the melody. She retrieved her bonnet, grabbed the lace shawl she had brought for the wedding, and was tying the bonnet ribbons under her chin when she met her aunt at the top of the stairs.

"Aunt Millicent, hurry and get your bonnet," Rosie said, pausing beside her aunt. "We are going to watch a race."

"A race?" Her eyes widened, and she smiled. "I so love to see horses run."

"Actually they are going to be driving carriages." Rosie adjusted the ribbons on her bonnet, which boasted blue velvet ribbons and white tulle inside the brim. It was the perfect match for her blue gauze gown, which was decorated with lace along the skirt and short, puffed sleeves. She settled the lace mantilla over her shoulders. "Sir Alexander challenged Mr. Byrne to prove that his carriage is swifter."

"Oh." Her smile vanished.

Rosie grabbed her aunt's hands, not willing to let her slip away again to hide behind a locked door. "Aunt Millicent, Sir Alexander sat almost across the table from me at breakfast. He is smart and kind and charming."

"That he is."

"But you are avoiding him, and you have not explained why. You asked for a tray in your room so you did not have to come to breakfast."

"Yes."

"Aunt Millicent—"

"Rosie!" Rupert's shout careened up from the foyer. She looked over the rail to see him waving his hat at them. "We must leave if we want to be in position to see the end of the race."

"Go ahead," Millicent said, cupping Rosie's cheek.

"I will tell Rupert that you are coming, and we will wait for you."

"No, go ahead without me."

"Without you?"

Aunt Millicent gave her a quick hug. "My dear child, do not look at me with such amazement. You know that I am never going to allow you to find yourself in a situation where you risk your reputation. Today, you will be riding in an open carriage with our host among a half dozen other open carriages. You will be well chaperoned, and I will have a chance to finish the final touches to my gown for the wedding."

"And avoid Sir Alexander?"

"Go, and have a wonderful time."

Rosie wanted to insist that her aunt come with them but knew it was useless. Her aunt could be the most stubborn person she had ever met. Watching as her aunt went back into her room and shut the door, Rosie wanted to weep. No one should hurt as much as Aunt Millicent did now.

Her steps were heavy as she went down the stairs. Even her heart was weighted when she saw Rupert looking up at her while she descended the steps. She tried to smile, but it was impossible.

His own smile faded. "I collect, from your expression, that your aunt has decided not to watch the race."

"Aunt Millicent told me that she needs to finish some tasks before the wedding," Rosie said.

"Which will give her another opportunity to avoid Quinn as she has since his arrival."

"Yes."

"She will not have a good time during the wedding if she continues to act like this."

"No, she will not." She hesitated, then asked, "Do you have any idea how to smooth the differences between them?"

"It would help if I knew what they were."

"I cannot tell you."

His smile grew taut. "Rosie, if you believed that I would prattle like—"

"No! Of course not!" She grasped his hand, not caring that she was being bold. Aunt Millicent was hurting, and Rosie did not want that pain to infect Rupert as well. "You misunderstood me. I cannot tell you because I do not know. She has not told me anything."

"Then we must go without her and grant her this time alone. There is no other choice."

"No." She sighed. For a moment, she considered going to her aunt and sitting with her, but she guessed Aunt Millicent had locked her door again.

He bowed again, sweeping his beaver hat in front of him as if it had a plume and he was a courtier. "Miss Dunsworthy, your carriage awaits beyond yon door."

"Why, thank you, my lord," she answered in the same light tone. Rupert clearly wanted to free her from the dismals, and she was glad to let him help her escape them.

Rosie put her hand on his arm as she walked with him out the front door. It was a lovely day, fresh with the scents of autumn and warm enough to watch the race in comfort. She thanked him when he assisted her into his open carriage. When Rupert climbed in and picked up the reins, she put her hands over his to halt him from giving the horse the signal to go. Hastily, she pulled her fingers away as she saw the grin he flashed her.

"Please say nothing to anyone about Aunt Millicent," she said in a near whisper.

"You can trust me."

"Yes, I know I can."

"Then trust me, Primrose."

She grimaced, and he laughed.

Slapping the reins lightly, he steered the carriage along the long avenue. "Then shall we be off to the race?"

"It seems that we are." She smiled as they passed through the gate and onto the road, turning in the opposite direction they had taken to Bath. She added nothing that might reveal the jumbled state of her heart.

Rosie listened as Rupert entertained her with

tales about events along the small side roads they passed. He seemed delighted that she was as interested in the history of the area as she was in the ancient tablets.

When he pointed to a mound in a field, he said, "That is where some of the Roman artifacts have been found. It merits further exploration."

"What fun you shall have!"

"You are welcome to join me in that exploration, if you wish."

"That is kind of you."

"But?"

"Aunt Millicent and I need to return to Dunsworthy Dower Cottage. We cannot leave the care of Barley and the cats to our neighbors simply because I want to poke into the ground to unearth some ancient coins."

"An excellent excuse to tell me no."

"Mayhap, but it is the truth, Rupert."

"Uh-huh."

"And what do you believe the truth is if you do not believe what I am saying?"

He looked at her steadily. "I think you are so close to revealing the real Primrose Dunsworthy that you fear if you stay here much longer, she will come out."

"The *real* Primrose Dunsworthy?"

"The one who sings with such passion and cares so much about others that she worries about them more than she does herself. The one who will say whatever she wishes whenever she wishes without fear of the consequences. The one who is not afraid of her own emotions."

"You are bereft of your senses."

"Quite to the contrary. I would say I am speaking with a clear mind." He stretched his arm along the back of the seat, his fingers brushing her nape. "I am willing to own that, since meeting you, I have needed to reconsider many opinions that I have long held. Mayhap you should do the same."

Rosie stared straight ahead. She could not ignore the sweet caress of his fingertips. Question what she had believed to be true? She was doing that endlessly. As each day had passed, and she had seen desire glowing in his eyes, she found it hard not to bring his lips to hers.

When his arm curved around her waist, she stiffened. Instantly he drew his arm away. She wanted to tell him that she was reacting not to him but to her own desires, which urged her to forget caution and raise her lips to meet what she was certain would be the rapture waiting on his.

Not looking at her, he gave her no hint to his thoughts as he said, "I fear we are already late." He shouted to the horses, which began to move more smartly along the road.

"Yes, I fear we are."

"For the race only." He glanced at her and smiled. "I think we are just at the beginning of many other things."

She nodded. Denying the sensations whirling through her would be stupid. A sense of indescribable joy filled her as she no longer fought her own feelings. Music swelled through her head, a tune sweeter than any she had ever imagined before. With it came words that spoke of daring to fall in love and letting inhibitions fly away.

The carriage bounced in and out of a chuckhole so quickly that Rosie feared a wheel would pop off.

She yelped and asked, "Do you think we are watching the race or are part of it?"

Rupert laughed. "Sorry. I do not want to miss the beginning of the race. Nor do I want to be caught on this road when my uncle and Quinn are careering neck-or-nothing toward the finish line."

"You are very pleased with all of this."

"Yes."

"Why?"

"This is the first time in months my brother and his fiancée have spoken of anything other than their wedding."

Now it was Rosie's turn to laugh. "You have your uncle's pride to thank for that."

"I have to own that I am surprised Uncle Victor accepted such a wager. He is inordinately proud of his new carriage, and I cannot imagine him risking it simply to have the better of Quinn."

"It was Henry's suggestion that they have this race to prove which vehicle is faster."

"It seems my brother, too, may have been very eager to speak of something other than the wedding." A horn sounded in front of them. "By thunder, they are getting ready to begin the race." He slapped the reins, and the horses leaped forward.

Rosie grabbed the side of the carriage. "Slow down! You will get us killed before the race even starts."

"I—"

The carriage bounced wildly as it hit another hole. A shriek burst from her when the wheel did not drop back to the ground again. The horses whinnied a warning as they ran even faster, frightened by the out-of-control carriage bouncing behind them.

She lost her grip on the side and slammed against Rupert. Wrapping her arms around his waist, she held on as he put one arm around her to keep her from sliding away again. He twisted the reins around his other arm and fought to keep the carriage from flipping onto its side. Metal protested, and she huddled against him.

"Back on the ground," she whispered. "Get back on the ground."

As if the wheel had heard her, it dropped onto the road. The carriage bounced so hard she feared it would tip over in the other direction. Then it settled onto the road and continued along as if nothing had happened.

"Are you all right?" Rosie whispered, hoping it was only her head that was spinning and not the carriage.

"Yes." He loosened the reins from around his arm and shook his hand even as he was slowing the horses to walk. Welts were already rising along his skin.

"Oh, my." She touched one.

"Ouch! Are you trying to make it worse?"

"I wanted to be certain nothing was broken."

He wiggled his fingers. "See? It is fine."

"Good." She started to draw away. When he did not release her, she asked, "Do you mind?"

"Not a bit." He grinned, adjusting his arm so she faced him as she leaned across his chest, her eyes only inches from his mouth.

"Then please release me." Her voice was more breathless than she intended. Breathless in the wake of the near crash, she tried to tell herself, but lying to herself did not change the fact that the firm wall of his chest cradled her so wondrously. She could not keep from recalling how the pulse of anticipation had raced through her when she had thought he had been about to kiss her in the garden.

"Not until—" The carriage bounced again as he eased it back to the center of the road. With a chuckle, Rupert said, "Not until we are safely on our way again."

"Which I believe we are."

When he drew away his arm, she edged over to her side of the seat. She grimaced and brushed dirt off her skirt.

"You are welcome," Rupert said.

In surprise, she looked over at him. "For what?"

"For saving you from crashing into the side or falling onto the floor or soaring out of the carriage altogether."

"I did not ask for a hero."

"You did not have to. I thought I would step up and do the job. Sometimes a knight in shining armor does not have the time to wait to be asked if the lady wishes his help or if she wants to handle the situation on her own."

"Rupert, I am sorry." She knew she was blushing as she added, "I should have thanked you right away."

"Or you could have told me that I am a fool for driving at such a speed." He gave her a smile. "I am sorry, too. Let's get to the starting line so we can warn Uncle Victor about these chuckholes."

"And Sir Alexander?"

"Mayhap."

"Rupert!"

"Primrose!" he fired back in the same aghast tone.

She loosened her stiff shoulders and smiled. "You are jesting with me again."

"A most pleasurable pastime, I must own. You know I will warn Quinn as well. I do not want either man to come to a bad ending with this race."

"Or their passengers?"

He took his gaze from the road to stare at her. "Passengers? What passengers?"

"You told Ophelia that—"

"I told her that my uncle wished her to ride in his carriage but did not say in the race."

"She assumed that."

"Then I suspect Uncle Victor has set her to rights by now."

Rosie nodded but did not reply. How easily Rupert had manipulated Ophelia! Had he done the same to her as well? And if he had . . . when had he treated her thusly? She did not want to believe he had maneuvered her into his arms as readily as he had Ophelia into his uncle's carriage.

There must be a way to ask him that without offending him, but she had not found it by the time they reached the area where the carriages were gathering to watch the race's conclusion. She waved back to Jenna, who wore the widest grin Rosie had ever seen. Until now, Rosie had not guessed how much both Jenna and Henry were being worn down by the wedding preparations.

Rupert halted the carriage and stepped out. He held his hand up to her as she slid across the seat. As soon as she put her hand on his broad palm, she knew it had been a mistake when she was trying to keep her composure. His fingers closed over hers in a flesh trap. Trap? It could only be a trap if she did not want her hand in his, and she did yearn for his touch. Even this simple one created a mind-withering anticipation that defined thrilling. She did not try to pull away. She knew it would be useless to fight her own longings when combined with his, and she would be foolish to be drawn into a battle she could not win.

"Thank you," she said when she stood on the ground.

"That gratitude sounds even more grudging than when I kept you from flying out of the carriage."

"I told you that I am not accustomed to being rescued."

"I did not think so, but you must own that today you did need help."

"I would not have needed rescue if you had not driven as rapidly as the Mail goes through Dunstanbury." She laughed. "So do not take ideas into your head that I am happy that I needed to be rescued today."

He gave her another of those lingering looks that seared her. With his brow arched to a rakish angle, he said, "Too late. I already have ideas."

"Then mayhap you should rid yourself of them."

Walking with her toward the road where his uncle was checking the wheels of his carriage while Quinn sat impatiently in his, he chuckled. "'Tis not that easy to give such thoughts *congé* from one's mind."

"No one said it would be."

He paused in front of her and leaned on his hand against a tree inches from her bonnet.

"We shall miss the race," Rosie said, "if you persist with these antics."

Rupert fought not to smile. She was skittish today. His longing to smile disappeared. Was it just her aunt's dismay at Quinn's arrival that was bothering her or was it something else altogether? She had quivered in his arms and not just with the fear of being upset in the carriage. Even though she had tried to hide it, he had seen the glow in her eyes when he held her against him.

Or had it been no more than the reflection of his own craving? Mayhap she was the wiser, for she was now chatting with Jenna as if it had been Rosie's idea to have this race.

His brother gripped his arm. "This is just the dandy, isn't it?"

"I understand the whole of this was your idea."

"Yes, and as I said, 'tis a dandy one. We get to watch a well-matched race on this lovely day with two lovely ladies." He lowered his voice. "And we escape from the house before Jenna's mother can find something else that needs to be decided immediately."

"Now I understand. I . . . Good day, Dunsworthy." Rosie's cousin chuckled. "I am seeking advice."

"On what?" Henry said, smiling even more broadly.

"Which one do you think will win? I am not as familiar with either driver as you are."

Rupert was glad to leave the two men talking but realized as he looked around that Rosie had vanished into the crowd edging both sides of the road. His smile faded when he saw her still standing with Jenna, but another woman had joined them.

Ophelia!

He cursed under his breath. Even from where he stood, he could see Ophelia's triumphant expression and Rosie's closed one. Jenna was wringing her hands in obvious dismay.

Not waiting to collect his brother, who would be irritated to see Jenna distressed, Rupert strode to where the three women stood. He was not in the least surprised when Ophelia suddenly cooed and wrapped her arm around his. He no longer thought the way she held his arm, pressing it to her lush breast, was inadvertent. Ophelia was single-minded, and she wanted him to be the same.

Humiliating her was the last thing he wished to do, but she was making it more and more difficult to disentangle himself from her eager clutches. He slowly drew his arm away as if he had no more on his mind than lifting his hat as he greeted the three women. He looked at Rosie, but her gaze was focused on Ophelia.

*Like any prey waiting for its pursuer to strike,* he thought. It was time for Ophelia to learn that she could not ride roughshod over anyone who stood between her and what she wanted.

"The race is about to begin," he said in a purely conversational tone. "Jenna, I know Henry has saved a spot for you near the starting line."

She gave him a grateful smile. "Thank you. I . . ." Her face displayed how she was torn between running to her betrothed and staying to protect Rosie from more of Ophelia's barbed comments.

"Ophelia," he went on, keeping his smile in place, "Uncle Victor is sure to want to see his good luck charm before he begins the race."

"I wished him luck already," Ophelia answered as she gave him a scintillating smile.

"Mayhap he does not believe it is enough now that he has examined Quinn's phaeton at close quarters."

"He was asking for me?"

Lying was uncalled for, although it would have been the simplest course. Instead he said, "You know how happy he always is to see you."

"As I am to see you." She leaned toward him, that seductive smile aimed directly at him.

He did not have to look past her to know that Rosie would be trying to slip away unnoticed. If he did not bring this skimble-skamble conversation with Ophelia to a close immediately, Rosie would flee rather than speak the thoughts that he suspected were in her head.

"The race is about to begin," he said and gave Ophelia a gentle shove toward where Uncle Victor was climbing into his carriage. "Hurry, or you will be too late."

"Will you wait for me?"

"You will see me about."

She hurried away, pausing only to blow him a kiss.

"Don't," Rupert murmured without turning. "Don't go, Rosie, please."

Rosie halted as she was about to walk in the other direction. When Rupert faced her, she tried to make her own face blank. It was impossible.

"You need to stop letting her get the upper hand," he said.

"I will not sink to her level of cattiness."

"Do you expect her to be impressed with your exemplary manners?" He laughed as he held out his arm. "She seems doomed to fail such a lesson."

She hesitated, wondering what trouble Ophelia would create if the brunette saw her on his arm.

Rupert did not allow her to make up her mind. He picked up her hand and placed it securely in the crook of his arm. When he tilted her face so she could see his smile, he winked at her.

She grinned, unable to hide this happiness. She liked the way he made her believe everything was perfect because she was with him. He brought humor and a challenging wit into her life that had been so quiet before she met him.

He led her toward the edge of the road where they could watch the beginning of the race. Her happiness lasted only as long as it took to walk to the road, for Ophelia turned to scowl at them.

Ophelia's furious expression caught many eyes, for other guests began to stare. As Rosie's face grew warm, she wondered if she would have been smarter to stay back at the house with Aunt Millicent.

"Do not let her ugly glower ruin your day," Jenna said as she and Henry came to stand next to them. "If she keeps wearing it, her face will freeze that way."

Rosie laughed. She could not halt herself, even though she was inviting more rage from Ophelia. When she sat beside Jenna on a hummock, Rupert and Henry squatted behind them. She forgot about Ophelia as Rupert pointed out the differences in the two carriages.

"Which one do you believe will win?" she asked.

"Quinn's. No question."

Henry chuckled. "I suspect you are right, but it will be fun to see for ourselves. Don't you think so, Jenna?"

Her answer went unheard beneath the shrill cacophony of a horn.

Rosie cringed as the carriages scurried past at an unbelievable speed. Wiping dust away from her face, she coughed. She heard shouts all around her.

Her hand was grabbed. Yanked to her feet, she gasped, "What are you doing, Rupert?"

He led her at her top pace to his carriage. Tossing her up onto the seat, he jumped in beside her. "We have to take the shortcut to reach the finish line so we can see the end of the race."

"That is crazy!"

"It most definitely is." He set the horses back in the direction they had come. "And a great deal of fun!"

Gripping the side of the carriage, which seemed to be going at the same breakneck speed as the racers, Rosie laughed and waved when other carriages passed them. Shouts and cheerful jeers flew from one carriage to another. When she heard someone singing a lighthearted song, she began to hum it and discovered that its tempo was perfect for this swift journey.

When Rupert began to sing along with the others, she smiled. His voice when he sang possessed the same rich warmth as when he spoke. Her own firm soprano harmonized easily with his baritone. As they continued to sing, a slow smile spread across his face.

As the music came to a close, Rosie said, "I did not know that you sang so well, Rupert."

"You don't know many things about me."

"That is true. I know you love to try to solve the puzzle presented by ancient artifacts, and I know that you hold your brother and the rest of your family in high esteem. There is no other reason that you would have taken time from your studies for this wedding otherwise."

"I stand corrected." He chuckled. "Or should I say that I sit corrected? You seem to know me well." He turned the carriage onto a narrow road.

"The others are going the other way." She looked at the cloud of dust along the main road.

"Not all of them will. Henry knows this route, too, for we explored it often as lads."

Although Rosie wanted to look back to make sure Henry and Jenna were following them on this narrow, tree-edged road, doing so would suggest she did not trust Rupert. Again she wanted to laugh sadly. She could trust him. Just not herself when she was so close to him, for her thoughts were of what they could share along this lane that dappled with shade from the trees poking out of the hedgerows.

"You sing very well, too, Primrose." He held up one hand before she could protest. "I mean, Rosie."

"You are developing very bad habits. I shall have to check with Henry and discover if there is a name that you despise as much as I do that one."

"A wasted chore. If I can survive the name Rupert, you can be certain that no other epithet would ever disturb me." He flashed her a smile. "I am pleased to hear you singing again. You sing so well."

"We often sing together at Dunsworthy Dower Cottage, especially now that Bianca is not there to entertain us with her stories."

His arm, which had been resting along the back of the seat, slipped down so his fingers could curve around her shoulder. Gently he pulled her closer. When she tried to draw away, he laughed. "Don't be frightened of me."

"If someone was to see—"

"No one shall see." He did not release her as he added, "Do you know this tune?"

When he began to sing, she did not join in. He was trying to use her love of music to woo away her good sense. Yet, the song was innocent, and there could be no harm in singing. She let the melody flow out of her heart as she waved to Jenna and Henry when they drove on the other side of the trees to pass Rupert's carriage.

"Hurry!" shouted Henry. "I want to see which one wins."

Rupert smiled without missing a note as his

brother's carriage bounced back onto the lane and sped away. Upon finishing the song, he told Rosie to choose another. They laughed as she tried to pick an old song he knew. Then he suggested they sing a popular one that she had never heard. The beat of the horses' hoofs provided an undertone to their singing. Entwining with the fresh scents along the lane, their music seemed to fit the day as readily as the birds' trills.

Rupert smiled as he began yet another song as the carriage slowed going up a hill. Merrily she sang the bright melody without paying attention to the words. Only when she realized that he had stopped singing did she pause.

He pulled the buggy to the side of the road, and said softly, "Sing that last verse again."

"Rupert, we shall miss the end of the race."

"We shall be there in time. Sing me that last verse again."

"Don't you know it?"

He brushed a strand of hair back beneath her bonnet, setting her cheek aflame. Not with embarrassment, but with elation at his bewitching touch. "Please, just sing it for me one more time."

"Rupert, I—"

"Humor me. Sing it."

Baffled, she did. It was only when she reached the last line that she discovered his intent. Her voice faded as she sang, "Kiss me once, then kiss me again."

He stroked her shoulders and down her arms to her elbows. Cupping them, he whispered, "As you have asked . . ." His lips brushed hers lightly. "That is the once."

"Rupert, you are being absurd!" She put up her hands to push him away, but when they settled on his shoulders, they betrayed her by stroking the brawny muscles beneath his coat.

"Why not? I think you are far too serious, Rosie. I think you need to be more absurd." He ran his finger across her lip, which quivered in anticipation of his touch. "As you asked with your song, I have kissed you once." His voice dropped to a husky whisper, "Now again."

His arm swept her to him. When his mouth covered hers this time, there was nothing fleeting about his kiss. It demanded all the rapture he was offering her. Boldly, he stroked her lips with his tongue, leaving liquid fire to burn in its wake. Caught within the yearning she could not—did not want to—control, she let her fingers sift up through his dark hair. She wanted to keep his mouth against hers until she had savored every bit of the joy.

He raised his lips from hers, and she whispered, "No!"

"No to my kiss or no to stopping?"

"No to stopping." She steered his mouth to hers again.

His arm tightened around her, thrilling her with myriad sensations as he pressed her to his unyielding chest. Only when the distant sound of a carriage intruded did he release her.

Taking her hands in his, he whispered, "My sweet Primrose, we must go to the finish line for the race. To stay here might . . ."

"I know." She straightened her bonnet, which had been knocked awry by his fervor.

"After the race, we have much to talk about." He gave her that roguish grin that made her heart beat even more rapidly. "And more not to talk about."

As he picked up the reins with one hand and put

the other around her waist, she leaned her head against his shoulder. She could not wait to talk to him and *not* to talk to him again. She hoped it would be soon.

# CHAPTER FOURTEEN

The results of the three mile race surprised no one, except mayhap Victor Byrne. Sir Alexander's phaeton beat his by almost a quarter mile. Many glasses were raised in tribute to Sir Alexander's victory, and the bets were paid up with good humor.

If Mr. Byrne was distressed at his loss, he showed no sign of it. He seemed focused on monopolizing Ophelia's attention while Ophelia was doing all she could to draw Rupert into the conversation.

Rosie waited among the others in the foyer while Sir Alexander had collected his winnings and his huzzahs. When he turned to her, she guessed he had sensed her gaze on him.

"Yes, miss . . . ?"

"Dunsworthy," she replied.

His face lost its buoyant smile. When he motioned toward a corner by the stairs, she followed him there, glad to be able to ask her questions without other ears listening.

He was blunt. "You must be related to Millicent Dunsworthy."

"Yes, she is my aunt."

"Am I to believe that she is here as well?"

"Yes." She took a deep breath, fighting back the urge to end this conversation here, but she knew she could not make matters worse. "She is avoiding you."

"You most definitely are her niece, for you speak as candidly as she did when I first made her acquaintance."

"I care about my aunt, Sir Alexander."

"As I always have." His blue eyes dimmed with what she suspected was regret. That guess was confirmed when he added, "That is why I will respect her desire not to see me."

"If you spoke to her . . ."

"I would not know what to say after all these years."

"'How are you, Millicent?' might be a good place to start."

He patted her arm. "That is true, but it is not always the best place for starting over." He turned away, then said, "Please do tell your aunt that I still live in the same house on Grosvenor Square, and that I am well and hope she is the same."

Rosie nodded, recognizing his dismissal. She clenched her hands by her sides as he went to rejoin his comrades. She had been sure that Aunt Millicent was the most stubborn person in all of England, but it appeared Sir Alexander was her match.

"Lingering in corners is the perfect place for a wallflower." Ophelia looked down her nose at Rosie. "I am surprised that you are still here. A blue stocking like you usually avoids any gathering."

"I do not wish to draw daggers with you, Ophelia."

"Ah, listen to the country mouse trying to use Town cant. What a jolly!" Her smile was cold. "Do you say little because you do not want to show your ignorance of the ways of the Polite World, or is it simply that you have nothing worthwhile to say?"

Before she could answer, Mrs. Wallace said sharply, "Some people do not believe it necessary to air their vocabulary at every opportunity, Ophelia."

The brunette stiffened and scowled at Jenna's mother. Ophelia turned and walked away . . . as far as to where Rupert was standing. She slipped her arm through his and rested her head on his shoulder.

Rosie waited for him to ease away. When he did not, she swallowed roughly. He had drawn her into his arms and kissed her so eagerly not more than two hours ago. Now he was letting Ophelia slither along him like a harlot.

She mumbled, "Excuse me, Mrs. Wallace."

"Miss Dunsworthy, do not let Ophelia distress you."

"I am not distressed with Ophelia," she said as softly.

She should trust Rupert, and she did, but she could not comprehend the peculiar ways of the *ton*. Ophelia was right. Rosie would never fit in to the Polite World, and that was Rupert's world.

When she had accepted Jenna and Henry's invitation to attend their wedding, she had looked forward to seeing Rupert, mostly because she could not wait to discuss antiquities with him, for they had had little time to speak of that during the gathering at Henry's house.

But she scarcely thought of those tablet fragments now. She was, as Ophelia had pointed out maliciously, a country mouse. Among these forgiving guests, she had not yet made a grievous *faux pas*. The rest of the Polite World would not be forgiving, and she could bring shame to Rupert and his family if she became connected with them.

Connected?

How could she use such an unfeeling word to describe her longings to have Rupert hold her again in his arms as he whispered that he ached for her, too? She had thought such kisses meant he truly cared for her as he cared for no other woman.

She flinched. She had let Constable Powers kiss her. Mayhap he had believed the same of her. She was too confused to linger among the other guests. She was most certain to be unable to utter a single word.

Gathering her skirts, Rosie rushed up the stairs. She was, for once, glad Aunt Millicent's door was closed. Shutting her own quietly so she did not alert her aunt that she had returned, she went to the writing table by the bay window that matched the one in Rupert's book-room on the lower floor. She sat and pulled out the top drawer. From it she pulled the page where she had written the lines for the song that filled her mind.

*The seasons turn, and color is born once more on the trees;*
*All too soon it will be gone, leaving nothing more than memories.*
*Memories of red and gold and sunlight and a bird's lingering song,*
*Memories of a gentle wind from the sea to warm the heart through the winter long.*
*My heart is cold without you, when you are far from me and home.*
*I wonder why you have left me unkissed and without your arms around me and . . .*

"And then let another hold you," she whispered, crumpling up the page and shoving it back into the desk. She folded her arms. Putting her head down on the desk, she wished she had never come to Fortenbury Park. Try as hard as she could, she was unable to understand the Polite World and, for the first time, she was unsure if she wanted to.

Rosie was amazed how simple it was to avoid everyone. Although the house was crowded with guests, few ventured out into the raw, damp afternoon. The wind swirled through the branches, luring leaves to come and join its dance before leaving them to drift to the ground.

As she walked along the wall that followed the contour of the hill, Rosie stared down at the roofs of Bath. She thought of the people who lived beneath them. They were going about their lives while she was questioning everything in hers.

She paused by a bench that served as a stile. Sitting on it, she clasped her hands around the book she carried. She had brought it with her in case someone had asked her what she was intending to do. She could say how she wanted to be alone to read, and the other guests would have respected her yearning for quiet. No one had asked.

But she had not walked past the gardens to look for a nook to read. She had left the house in order to discover a place where she could think without interruption.

Only one thing could she think about. Aunt Millicent had been baffled and hurt by love. Now Rosie was suffering the same. Both of them had let the swirl of the *ton* beguile them, and now both of them were draped in sadness.

*Once, twice, thrice—*
*Be it by heaven or by the devil's own device,*
*What joy or grief for one shall be worthy,*
*Shall come the same for each Dunsworthy.*

Rosie's head snapped up as the thought of the carving on the side of the Dunstanbury Church wafted through her head.

"No!" she whispered. If she was foolish enough to believe that, she would be condemning Bianca to sorrow, too. That could not be what the saying meant. Bianca had found joy and love. Lord Dunsworthy was announcing his plans to wed, so he must have found joy and love, too. So, if one accepted the old legend, Rosie and Aunt Millicent should find joy and love as well. Mayhap they simply had sought love among the wrong people. Mayhap they should have looked no farther than the borders of the shire.

"Miss Rosie?"

Coming to her feet, Rosie stared in disbelief as Constable Powers hurried toward her. His clothes were covered with dust and showed the wear of the long journey from Dunstanbury.

"Constable Powers! What are you doing here?"

He did not answer. Rather he stepped toward her, backing her up against the wall as he had at the cottage. She kept the book in front of her, a paltry shield, but the only one she had.

"I thought it would be obvious why I am here," he replied.

"You were able to get the stolen horses back?"

"Yes, but those tidings could have waited until you returned to Dunstanbury." His eyes narrowed. "*If* you returned to Dunstanbury."

She frowned back at him. "What are you talking about? Aunt Millicent and I are coming home once the wedding celebrations are past. Moss will be taking us there, just as we planned."

His shoulders sagged, and the fierce frown left his face. When he spoke, his voice was once again the kindly one she knew so well. "I am pleased to hear that, Miss Rosie. I had thought you might change your mind once you sampled the dazzling life lived by fancy folks."

"It is a tempting life." She looked back at the massive house. She could easily imagine living with Rupert in it. No, she could easily imagine living with Rupert at the Dunsworthy Dower Cottage, where they could spend their time in study and discussion . . . and enjoying luscious kisses. Living at Fortenbury Park with him took more imagination because she had gone into only a small portion of its many rooms.

"Tempting is what it is." Constable Powers's voice drew her attention back to him, and she realized he was staring at her. "But such a place is not for the likes of us. I know you are the late baron's daughter, but you belong in Dunstanbury. You are not like the people who parade from the country to London and back again over and over."

"There are just as many different sorts of people among the *ton* as there are in our parish."

"Mayhap, but they are not the same as we are. Most of them have never done anything for themselves." He paused as an open carriage drove by on the road at the far edge of the field. Laughter and buoyant conversation floated out from it. Waving aside the dust carried to them on the wind, he said, "They only entertain themselves and each other in an endless circuit of parties here and there."

She could not argue with what he said, even though she wanted to come to the defense of those she now considered friends. Jenna and Henry thought only of their wedding, not of the work that it required of the many servants who were trying to make their wishes come true. Ophelia could think of nothing but marrying and marrying to gain a title. Even Rupert had the leisure to study his fragments and try to decipher the symbols on them.

"You know it is true," the constable continued when she did not reply. "If they were without their servants, they would be lost."

"Some of them—"

"I agree there are some who would be able to survive, but none of them have ever gotten their hands dirty."

"Rupert has."

Constable Powers frowned. "Rupert?"

"Lord Fortenbury," she hurried to reply.

"I know whom you meant, but I was not aware you spoke of him so."

"He gave me permission to address him by his given name at the same time he asked if he might use mine."

"And you told him yes?" Dismay filled the constable's eyes.

Too late she realized that she had never offered him the same permission. He had never asked.

He shook his head as he sighed. "Can't you see that you are being bewitched by the life they live? Will you ever be happy in Dunstanbury again?"

"You are being silly. Dunstanbury has always been my home."

"But can you be happy there again? Can you marry a man without a title other than constable?"

She stared at him in astonishment. Constable Powers wanted to marry her? She knew he must. She had known it from the moment he drew her into his arms and kissed her, even though she had tried not to think of it. Davis Powers would never toy with a woman's heart by kissing her and then allow another woman to drape herself over him. He spoke plainly, and he was content with the simple life he would have once he passed along his constable duties at year's end to the next volunteer. He would spend his time on his few acres, growing food for his table and raising sheep and cows. So simple, so commonplace, so right for everyone in Dunstanbury.

She was not sure it was right for her. From her earliest memories, she had longed to wander far beyond the village's borders. Through her reading, through her sister's stories, through her music, she had escaped for an afternoon or an evening. Until now, she had assumed she would live out her days in the small village.

Constable Powers grasped her arms and pulled her closer. The book thudded against his chest, but he did not release her. "Is it too late?" he asked.

"I don't know." She could not be false with him, but she doubted he would understand how her dreams had led her to distant places all her life.

"Could you stay with me in Dunstanbury?"

"I appreciate your offer, but—"

"You want to marry someone else."

She met his eyes as she whispered, "I don't

know." Her heart pushed her to fantasize about being with Rupert for the rest of their lives. Listening to it would be foolish, especially when she had seen how he kissed her and a short time later let Ophelia cling to him. She wanted a man who loved her completely and set aside other women.

*A man like Constable Powers.* It would have been perfect if she loved him, but she did not. He was a friend, as he had always been. Nothing more.

"You must fight its appeal," the constable urged. "Don't you see? First there are the small things like using given names, then you are seduced more and more by the *ton.*"

"You speak with rare authority," said Rupert from the far side of the wall.

Rosie felt the heat rising on her cheeks, but Constable Powers's were bleached. As Rupert climbed over the stile to stand beside them, she wondered how much he had heard. She gasped as she realized the constable still held her close to him. She stepped back. For a long moment, she thought he would not let her go. What would happen if he did not? She could not guess, and she was very relieved when he drew aside his hands.

Taking another step away, she bumped into the wall. The book fell from her hands.

Rupert bent to pick it up. When he tilted it to see the title, his dark brows rose. He said nothing as he handed it to her, but she was sure he was appalled to see dampness on the book he had purchased in London and not yet read.

"Thank you," she managed to whisper.

He nodded toward her, then turned to the constable. "I am amazed, Constable Powers, to see you so far from your parish. Can I hope your appearance at Fortenbury Park is the harbinger of glad tidings?"

"Your horse has been found, my lord." Constable Powers met Rupert's eyes steadily. "Along with Lord Wandersee's horses."

"Where were they found?"

"The thieves tried, as we had suspected they might, to sell them at a market day in the next parish. They were not clever men. Just greedy ones, because they even claimed the horses were fine enough to belong to a lord." Constable Powers gave the faintest smile. "They were taken quickly to the local justice of the peace while the horses were given into my care."

"I am very pleased to hear that. You are to be commended, Constable Powers."

"I brought all the horses with me, and I left them at the stable. None of them were injured."

"Your dedication to your duty is exemplary, Constable Powers. I will see you get the reward I told you I would offer for the return of the horses."

"Reward?" asked Rosie before she could halt herself.

"Ten pounds," Rupert replied.

Her eyes widened. Such a generous reward would be a windfall for the constable. No wonder the constable had come to Fortenbury Park to claim it. When she looked at Constable Powers, he was regaining his color.

"Plus half that amount again, Constable Powers," Rupert said, "for your time in bringing the horses here. That was something I did not expect."

"I was glad to do that, my lord. There was no reason for you to return to Dunstanbury to collect them."

"I appreciate your saving me the trip."

Rosie bit her lower lip as she listened to the two men parry with polite words. The constable had taken the time away from his other chores to return the horses personally so Rupert would have no excuse to come back to Dunstanbury. The men were using courtesy as well-sharpened foils aimed at the very heart with no quarter offered.

"If you go to the house, Constable Powers," Rupert added, "you will find an excellent meal for you in the kitchen. I will bring you your reward after I arrange for transportation for you back to Dunstanbury."

"There is no need for you to do that, my lord."

"Nonsense. It is my pleasure."

Constable Powers glanced again at her, then turned on his heel.

Rosie held the book in front of her again as she watched the constable walk away. Should she go after him and say—what? That she was sorry she could not love him as he wanted? He deserved a wife who adored him for the man he was, not a wife who had valued his friendship for many years and wanted to continue having it and nothing more.

"A good man," Rupert said.

"Really? You think so?"

"Why? Don't you?"

"Yes."

When she added nothing more, he frowned. "His efforts on our behalf have been extraordinary. As soon as I heard that the constable had come to the stable with the horses, I wanted to thank him personally. Moss will be relieved, and I must own to feeling the same that Osiris is back and is unhurt."

"Oh."

"Oh?" he repeated back to her. "What is wrong,

Rosie? If I intruded on something between you and the constable, something you wished to continue, you need only say so."

"No, there is no reason to say anything."

"I am glad." He ran his finger along the top of the book, and the memory of his touch flooded her with longing. "Very glad." He bent and kissed her lightly on the cheek.

"Rupert, you should not—"

"Hush," he commanded before his mouth caressed hers with tenderness.

She wanted to melt into his arms again, but one of them had to be sensible. She slipped out of his arms. "I cannot be hushed when I must speak up."

"On behalf of your dedicated swain?"

Again she clasped the book close, as she wished she was holding him. "Constable Powers is not my swain."

"But he wishes to be." He put his hands on her shivering shoulders. "Do you wish him to be?"

"You are asking a very personal question."

"I know. Will you answer it?"

"No."

He surprised her when he smiled. "I did not think you would."

"You should let me go," she whispered.

"Not yet. Not before you hear what I have to say."

"It is not what you have to say that worries me."

"But what you think I cannot keep from doing?"

She shuddered, for she feared unleashing the strong emotions in his ebony eyes. She released her breath in a gasp when he brought her fingers to his lips and kissed them gently.

"Forgive me, Primrose," he said with quiet dignity.

"Please, Rupert, do not jest with me now."

"If you will forgive me for being unable to resist the temptation of touching you."

She frowned, pulling her hand out of his. "I can only forgive you, Rupert, if it does not happen again while Aunt Millicent and I are your guests."

Rupert ran a single finger along her lips. When he smiled, she knew he did not believe that her protests were sincere. Why should he when she had to fight to keep from throwing her arms around him again?

"I make no promises when I know I may not be able to keep them," he said.

Turning away, she said, "Then I believe our best course is to avoid each other."

Abrupt sarcasm thickened his voice. "What a charming idea! We can be just like your aunt and Quinn and always avoid each other."

"They made their mistake long ago, and now they are paying the price for it. We should learn from their mistakes not to make another one."

"Do you think kissing me is a mistake?"

"Yes."

He stared at her, obviously not expecting such a reply. She grasped his hand, although she knew with every touch how she endangered her resolve to put an end to his sweet caresses.

"Rupert, we are only hoaxing ourselves."

"What are you saying?"

"You know what I am saying. There is a wide breach between the world you live in and the one I live in. I know Bianca was able to cross it, but I am not my sister."

"You have crossed it."

"No, I have only peered at the other side from

halfway across the bridge. Constable Powers's arrival reminds me of that."

"You care more about what others will think of you than anything else." All tenderness vanished from his face. "By thunder, Rosie, I thought you were different from Ophelia. You are just the same."

She wanted to cry out that he was mistaken, that she was nothing like Ophelia King, but he walked away toward the house before she could decide exactly what to say.

Dropping back to sit on the bench, she watched Rupert walk along the wall until he disappeared into the distance. She derided herself for not speaking up. And what could she have said? That she loved him and wished he loved her, too?

# CHAPTER FIFTEEN

"You look perfect," said Aunt Millicent as she viewed Rosie from every angle. "Save that you need to smile to complete your ensemble for tonight's ball."

"I will try." She stared at her reflection in the glass. The white gown's only decoration was a single pink rose in the center of the ribbon beneath her bodice. A matching garland of roses was twisted through her hair, and she could have been one of the fairy princesses in Bianca's stories.

*A fairy princess with no hope of a happy-ever-after ending,* she thought. She shook that thought from her head. Since she had come into the house from her walk, she had reminded herself again and again that she might never have another chance to attend a fancy assembly like the one to be held in the ballroom on the floor below. She needed to enjoy the evening.

Aunt Millicent drew on her kid gloves and sighed. "I hope my dreary spirits have not down-pinned you, Rosie."

"I cannot be truly happy if you are unhappy."

"You must not let my past ruin this evening for

you. Who knows when we will dance at a viscount's ball again?"

*Never!* She bit back that word before it could upset her aunt more. When she saw her aunt's sad expression in the glass, she turned and said, "Aunt Millicent, if there is anything—anything at all—that I can do to ease this evening, please let me help."

"I appreciate your offer, my dear Rosie." She kissed Rosie's cheek. "But I have decided that I do not wish to hide in the unchangeable past. It is time to put it aside and be grateful for the happiness I have with you and our lives at Dunsworthy Dower Cottage."

"If you need me—"

"I will put my fingers in my mouth and whistle for you."

Rosie laughed as she tried to imagine her gracious aunt doing something so out of hand.

"Keep that pretty smile," Aunt Millicent said.

"I shall, for I do not want you whistling at me if I fail to do so."

Laughing together, they walked out into the corridor. Rosie let the music from an orchestra guide them toward the great hall where the wedding eve ball was being held. Jenna would be there with her betrothed. Would she tell Henry how she had hidden for most of the day in Rosie's rooms so she could avoid her mother? Mrs. Wallace seemed about to have a *crise de nerfs* at every turn.

Rosie's feet faltered when she realized they would be passing Rupert's book-room. She had been grateful for Jenna's company, which had given her the perfect excuse to stay in her rooms . . . and avoid Rupert. She did not know what she could say to him to explain why she had apparently had such a change of heart. And she feared she could not keep from pleading with him to bring her into his arms again.

Knowing that she should keep her eyes focused on the corridor ahead of her, she glanced into the room. She drew in a sharp breath, and her aunt put a comforting hand on her arm, keeping her steps from faltering. Did Aunt Millicent know of Rosie's blunder that now haunted her? Odd to think of those wondrous kisses as a mistake, but they must have been. Not only her mistake, but Rupert's. Mayhap Aunt Millicent had made exactly the same mistake with the undeniably charming Sir Alexander.

Her steps slowed again as she stared at Rupert, who was bent over his desk. He was dressed more formally than she had ever seen him. His black coat was the sole color he wore. His shirt, cravat, waistcoat, and breeches were all an immaculate white.

She had seen him only once since yesterday, and he had greeted her with polite coolness when she joined her aunt and the other guests for last night's supper. Now her gaze was drawn to his hands, which were splayed across one of his tablets. His fingers touched the stones as gently as he had caressed her. *This* was what he loved. She was sure of that. If he had his way, she guessed he would spend the rest of his life digging in the Egyptian sands in hopes of finding the key to unlocking every bit of information he could about this past civilization.

That could not be, because he had the obligations of his title. He had said nothing that suggested he hated the restrictions placed upon him. Unlike his brother, who tried to control everything around him by making it just as he wished, Rupert accepted the destiny that was his and worked for a way to combine his duties and his studies.

"Rosie," hissed her aunt.

She nodded and followed Aunt Millicent past Rupert's book-room. The hope that Rupert would have taken note of her and would come out to ask her to wait so they could talk and clear the air between them vanished as she and her aunt went down the stairs.

The voices grew louder as they reached the wing that connected the great hall to the newer sections of the house. Rosie tried not to let her mouth gape when she entered the great hall, but she failed. Although all the guests must be within, the room did not seem crowded.

Narrow windows welcomed in the starlight to float among the intricate pattern of the rafters near the peaked roof. Two huge iron chandeliers, whose circumferences were as wide as carriage wheels, had dozens of candles lit. Under her feet, broad stones were smooth from many footsteps before hers.

Mrs. Wallace came forward, smiling broadly as she said, "Ah, here you are. Do come and sample the champagne. It is just as fine a vintage as I had hoped."

Rosie nodded, even as she heard her aunt swallow her laugh. Mrs. Wallace's expression announced that *everything* tonight was just has she had hoped . . . and planned.

When Aunt Millicent took two glasses from a tray carried by a passing servant, Rosie took a big sip.

"Slowly," chided her aunt. "That is the way to drink champagne."

Again Rosie nodded, turning as the orchestra began playing again. When she saw one of the musicians was seated at a dark rosewood piano, she walked closer to watch him play. Music filled her head, but it was a sorrowful song, unlike the one she had been trying to create words for. If she touched the piano keys, could she play something that would banish those sad notes from her head? But it was not the keys she longed to touch, but Rupert.

"He is ready to accompany you whenever you wish," Jenna said as she smiled at Rosie.

"Whenever I wish?"

"So you can sing for us."

"Me?" She pressed her hand over her heart, which seemed to have stopped at the thought of standing up in front of all the guests and singing. "I think you are mistaken, Jenna. I have no plans to sing tonight."

"You must! Mama told me that you would." She grasped Rosie's hands. "She said that Rupert mentioned that you would be delighted to sing for us on this special night."

"Rupert suggested I sing tonight?"

Furrows of concentration lengthened Jenna's round face. "I am sure that is correct. Who else would have suggested it?"

"Aunt Millicent," she replied, even though she knew that her aunt would not make such an offer. Aunt Millicent would not put Rosie into a situation where she was sure to end up as red as a hunting coat.

"No, I would have remembered if Mama said it was your aunt who suggested that you sing this evening." She motioned to the man at the piano. "Please accompany Miss Dunsworthy while she sings."

"Jenna, no!" Rosie gasped.

"Oh, please, Rosie. Mama says you sing beautifully."

"I never sang for—"

"Do sing for us!"

A sharp laugh came from behind her as Ophelia said, "Oh, leave her be."

Rosie turned, shocked, that Ophelia would come

to her defense. Ophelia was dressed in what appeared to be earthbound moonlight. Her gown glistened, and the jewels around her neck and in her hair seemed to possess a light source of their own.

Before Rosie could thank her, Ophelia went on, "She does not want to complete her humiliation by revealing that she was bragging about a talent that no country mouse could possess."

"Stop it!" cried Jenna.

Rosie clasped her hands in front of her as Jenna's raised voice silenced every other one in the great hall. Now Rosie had no doubts that each eye in the room was focused upon the three of them. Seeing Aunt Millicent pushing through the crowd, a horrified expression on her face, Rosie bit her lip. Jenna held out her hand to Henry, who rushed forward to take it. He was scowling at Ophelia.

As her eyes shifted toward the door, Ophelia's satisfied smile broadened. Rosie did not need to turn to see who stood in the doorway now. The possessive curve of Ophelia's lips told her that Rupert had entered the great hall.

"What is wrong?" Henry asked, distressed. "My dear Jenna, tell me what is amiss, and I shall do all I can to put it to rights."

"Henry, it is horrible how Ophelia is taunting Rosie. Ask her—"

"Yes," Ophelia said, "do ask Miss Dunsworthy to either sing or stop her mewling so we may dance. Rupert has arrived, and I do believe he promised the first dance to me." She flashed an arrogant, triumphant smile at Rosie.

Jenna put her hand on Rosie's arm. "Do not let her goad you into doing something you do not wish to."

Patting her friend's hand, Rosie looked to where Rupert still stood in the doorway. Her gaze locked with his, even though there were dozens of people between them. His face had little expression, as she wished hers did. Even from where he stood, he must know what was happening across the room. Whispers were flitting about the room like an insect, never settling in one spot and constantly buzzing.

Rosie smiled at Jenna and Henry, who had his arm around his betrothed as if he expected Ophelia to attack her physically. Without speaking, Rosie went to the piano. The man who had been playing stood and bowed to her as he offered to accompany her if she would tell him what she wished to sing.

"Thank you," she said quietly. "I shall play for myself."

"As you wish, miss." He stepped aside.

Ignoring the whispers that were growing louder and louder, Rosie adjusted the stool and sat. She began to play the introduction to one of the songs she and Rupert had sung during the race.

"You want us to believe you wrote *that*?" Ophelia's laugh soared over the music.

Henry leaned forward as Rosie stopped playing. "Sing the song you have written."

Rosie raised her fingers over the keys, then lowered them back to her lap. She had been working on the words to go with her song. She had not spent time practicing the music itself.

"You do not need to do this!" Jenna's eyes were filled with tears, and a single one fell down her cheek.

"I know." She took Jenna's hand and squeezed it. "It will be fine."

Another of Ophelia's derisive laughs stiffened Rosie's shoulders, but she forced them to ease as she raised her fingers over the keys again.

The room became silent, save for a single set of

footfalls crossing the stones. She did not look up from the keys as she re-created the page with the music's words in her mind. Yet she knew the footfalls belonged to Rupert. They did not pause as she played the first bar of the song that had begun lilting through her on the day he arrived in Dunstanbury.

Ceding herself to the music, she let her anger and hurt surge out of her fingers. The notes transformed it until she found the joy that emanated from the melody. She let it transfigure her as well, finding strength in each new fingering.

Then she began to sing. The words that had been so difficult to compose burst from her heart and past her lips.

*The seasons turn, and color is born once more on the trees;*
*All too soon it will be gone, leaving nothing more than memories.*
*Memories of red and gold and sunlight and a bird's lingering song*
*Memories of a gentle wind from the sea to warm the heart through the winter long.*
*My heart is cold without you, when you are far from me and home*
*I wonder why you have left me unkissed and without your arms around me and why I am now alone.*
*But I cannot be completely alone while I remember how my name danced each time you spoke it*
*In the moment before they found mine as I gave my heart to you knowing that if you broke it*
*All would be forgiven, for I remember on the day you gave me yours to hold within me*
*On the same precious day when we spoke our vows melding our hearts, you and I became we.*

The song was over before Rosie wished. She lifted away her fingers from the keys and took a steadying breath. The music took from her and strengthened her at the same time. It was her sanctuary as well as forcing her to bare her soul to all who heard it.

Applause erupted through the room along with cheers. She looked up from the piano, her gaze caught once again by Rupert's. He stood within the curve of the piano, not touching it.

"Brava! Brava!" came shouts from throughout the room.

"Sing another," Jenna said, the tears on her face now flowing past her smile. "That was wonderful, Rosie. Did you really write the song?"

"Yes." She did not look away from Rupert as she replied to Jenna. His eyes were hooded, so she could not guess what he was thinking. To own the truth, she did not know what *she* herself was thinking, for her thoughts were woven through the song, which had been incomplete until she let the words pour from her heart.

"I had no idea you were so talented," Jenna gushed. "What a perfect gift for Henry and me on the eve of our wedding."

The other guests surged forward to add their acclaim to Jenna's and Henry's. Mrs. Wallace stood behind her daughter, smiling so widely that everyone would know she had been behind the idea of Rosie singing.

Rosie whispered, "Thank you. That is very kind of you." She repeated it again and again, but, as the guests pressed closer, she put up her hands to keep from being smothered by their adulation.

A hand reached in front of her and closed the piano lid. With quiet authority, Rupert said, "Mayhap we shall be able to persuade Miss Dunsworthy to sing for us again tomorrow after the wedding. For now, it is time for my brother to dance with his beloved on the last night before they join their lives together." He turned to the orchestra and nodded before offering his hand to Rosie.

Her fingers quaked as they had not when she sang. She set them on his palm and closed her eyes as the thrill of his touch surged through her, as potent and as sweet as smuggled brandy. Opening her eyes, she gazed up at him while he drew her to her feet and past his guests who were clumped around the piano.

Behind them, the music swelled into a lyrical waltz. She gasped in astonishment when Rupert whirled her into his arms and into the rhythm of the dance. He said nothing as they spun amidst the other dancers, his arm tightening around her. As she gazed up at him, she hoped he was watching where they went. She was lost in his eyes. Her heart was lost as well because it had become his.

Her skirt twirled around his legs as they came to a halt along with the waltz. His fingers rose toward her face but froze when a sharp laugh came from behind her, followed by, "What else would a country mouse like her have had to do but write lovesick songs?"

Rosie spun and snapped, "Ophelia, you don't know what you are talking about."

Ophelia's eyes narrowed. "Do you think a country mouse like you should correct her betters?" Looking past her, she said, "Really, Rupert, I thought you would have explained to *all* your guests that proper behavior is expected. Even if *she* failed to learn, mayhap you could get through to her aunt, who at least had a taste of the *ton*."

"Enough!" Rosie closed the distance between her and Ophelia. "That is quite enough."

"Now, see here. *You* do not tell me what to do. You are not the mistress of Fortenbury Park."

"Nor are you." She knew she should say no more, but the words gushed from her, unstoppable, just as she had always feared they would if she did not restrain them. "Rupert has done everything he can to be gracious and polite to you, and you repay him by embarrassing him in front of his brother, Jenna, and all the guests for their wedding. And it is *their* wedding, not yours. Jenna and Henry should be the center of attention, not you. I do believe it is high time that you remembered that, Ophelia."

Aunt Millicent gasped as she rushed to Rosie's side, "Rosie, you should not speak so."

"That is right," seconded Ophelia with a shake of her thick, dark hair. "Listen to your aunt. She has some experience with the Polite World. You know nothing about how things are done among us, *Primrose.*"

With her hands in tight fists at her sides, Rosie knew she should withdraw. But if she did, would she ever again be willing to fight for something she wanted? "I do know how things are done among the *ton.* I am not a beef-head. I can see very clearly how you perceive your place in the Polite World. You are the one who seems unable to comprehend the facts that are right in front of your face." Again she warned herself to be silent before she demeaned herself completely by saying the wrong thing.

She could not.

It was as if she were a spectator, watching this brangle with Ophelia. She heard herself say, "No matter how many hints you drop, no matter how many rumors you start in the hope of having them spread throughout the *ton*, no matter how many of the guests you browbeat, the simple fact is that you are not getting married to Rupert this weekend. Mayhap he will ask you to be his wife." Her voice caught on that, but not enough to keep the words from continuing to fall from her lips. "Mayhap he will not, but it is *his* decision. Until he makes it, I trust that *you* can remember the canons of Society and desist with your childish antics."

"Childish?" cried Ophelia, her face twisting with fury. "I am not childish! Nor am I a country hobnail who is trying to destroy my reputation in order to enhance her own."

"I believe you have that backwards, Ophelia."

"Rosie!" gasped her aunt again, taking her by the arm. "You have said enough."

"Yes, I have." She nodded toward her aunt, then locked eyes with Ophelia again. "I have said everything I needed to say, and I hope, Ophelia, you have heard everything I have said."

"Do you think I need *your* advice on how to deal with men?"

"Mayhap not mine, but someone's. Good evening." Rosie turned and walked out of the great hall. The guests parted before her, their eyes wide. She heard the whispers behind her as the guests moved together again to share their shock at her words.

Then she was running along the corridor and up the stairs. She heard Rupert call to her. Pausing on the steps, she looked back.

He grasped the railing, slowly coming up the stairs. Did he fear that if he moved too quickly, she would turn and flee like the country mouse Ophelia had called her?

"You spoke your mind," he said as he paused two steps below her, so their eyes were almost even.

"But I should not have. I warned you about the words I try to keep silent. I simply could not keep them unspoken tonight."

"There is nothing wrong with that. You did not tell Ophelia anything she has not heard from many others, including me. She refused to heed us. Mayhap she will heed you, now that you have finally told her what you have kept in your heart."

"You can say that because . . . because . . ."

"Because my place in the *ton* is well-established?"

"No!" She stepped down one riser and gazed up at him. "Because you do not care what others think of you. You are very assured of who you are and what you want from life." Her tears blurred his face in front of her. "Even if you cannot always get it."

"If you think I pine for—"

"I am not speaking of any person, but of your dream of going to Egypt to see the ancient relics you have studied so intensely. To see them for yourself instead of reading of other people's descriptions. The Roman ruins around Bath have only whetted your yearning to see the far older ones along the Nile."

He stared at her as if he were seeing her for the first time. "How do you know that?"

"How can I *not* know that? Your very voice changes when you speak of hieroglyphics and your studies. It tells me of how desperately you adore your reading and your hopes of one day translating what is written on those tablets and your dreams of seeing with your own eyes what others write about."

"I did not guess I was translucent."

"You aren't." She paused so long that she thought he would say something. When he remained silent, too, she added, "You should not be surprised that others are as discerning as you are. After all, you quickly saw my delight with music."

"And then ruined your joy by speaking of my awe of your talent to Henry."

"Who told Mrs. Wallace."

"And she arranged with the orchestra for you to sing."

She hesitated, then said, "Jenna told me that you suggested I sing."

He gripped the railing so tightly that she feared his fingers would dig right into the marble. "You believed I would do that to you?"

"I want to say no."

"But you did."

This time, she was the one who turned and walked away. She could not endure the expression of betrayal on his face. He had trusted her, and she had vowed that she trusted him. She had believed she did.

Now she was unsure what she believed about anything.

The day of the wedding dawned with a hint of rain, but by the time Aunt Millicent came into Rosie's room, the sun was brushing aside the clouds. Aunt Millicent chattered about everything but what had happened in the great hall last night. She helped Rosie with her hair, which was entwined with a ribbon to match the white dress she had worn to the ball.

"Are you ready?" Aunt Millicent asked, tucking in a loose strand of Rosie's hair.

"Yes." Her voice had no more life than the stone walls.

"As soon as the wedding ceremony is over, Moss can take us back to Dunsworthy Dower Cottage."

"I know."

Aunt Millicent dampened her lips before saying, "That will give you some time to think about what you want to do."

"Do you think that will help anything?" she cried. "You have spent more than a decade in Dunstanbury, fleeing from what hurt you."

Cradling Rosie's face in her hands, Aunt Millicent whispered, "I was wrong. Do not make the same bumble-broth of your life."

"Wrong? Have you spoken with Sir Alexander?"

"I plan to today at the wedding."

Rosie hugged her aunt and tried to keep from sobbing. "I am so glad. If—"

A shout rang from beyond her door. She ran to it and flung it open. More shouts came from the lower floor.

Looking at her aunt, who shrugged, Rosie ran out into the hall. Out of all the voices, she could easily discern Rupert's with a sense that had little to do with her ears. She rushed down the stairs to where he was surrounded by Mrs. Wallace and the wedding attendants.

"What has happened?" she asked.

"They are gone!" Rupert replied, no longer startled at how glad he was to see Rosie. She might not be able to help with this muddle, but she strengthened him just by standing at his side. He did the same for her, because she had been brave enough to confront Ophelia's ridicule last night when he been beside her. Why had he failed to notice that before?

"Who are gone?" she asked.

"Henry and Jenna."

"Gone? Impossible!" Mrs. Wallace scowled at Rupert as if the whole of this were his doing. "No doubt the two of them are speaking in private somewhere."

"Before their wedding?" Rosie shook her head. "You know Jenna would not be seen on the day of her wedding by her bridegroom before the ceremony."

Rupert realized he was holding Rosie's hand. He was not sure if she had reached for his or if he had taken hers. Either way, her touch was exactly what he needed. He wanted to hold her hand and not let it go. Last night, he had sat in his book-room, but his thoughts had not been on his studies. Instead they had been on the constable, who had come all the way to Fortenbury Park for his reward. Not the money Rupert had offered, but for Rosie.

Too many times Rupert had let Rosie go, not wanting to overmaster her as Ophelia had tried to overmaster him. He had waited for her to believe she could trust him enough to speak her most precious thoughts, and he had begun to believe she might. Then he made a bumble-broth of everything by kissing her. He did not regret kissing her—how could he when her lips had been even sweeter than he had imagined?—but he was sorry she believed him to be no better than Ophelia, who cared more about marrying than whom she married.

There was no time to think of all that now, he reminded himself as he said, "And Henry has been determined to make this the most unforgettable wedding ever. He would not do anything now to endanger his opportunity to marry Jenna."

He was about to add more when Rosie put her other hand on his sleeve. The slightest nod of her head to the right told him that she wanted to speak with him privately. He gave orders to the servants, who were listening open-mouthed with astonishment. When he saw that neither Henry's manservant nor Jenna's abigail were among them, he strode away.

Leaving Mrs. Wallace to expound on the lack of co-operation she was receiving from the Jordan family's retainers in her search, he followed Rosie into the closest room—the dining room. It was empty, but she went to the door that led to the kitchen corridor. She put her ear to the door, then opened it. She left the door open a finger's breadth before she faced him.

He did not need to hear her speak to know that she wanted him to shut the door to the passage, where Mrs. Wallace's voice still was rising in dismay. He walked to where Rosie stood beside the far end of the table in front of the bay window.

He knew she had not brought him here to speak of what ached in his heart. The dullness left by the hurtful words they had spoken still dimmed her eyes. Yet, with the sunlight streaming through her auburn hair and outlining her alluring curves beneath her simple gown, she was immersed in a sumptuous glow that was impossible to ignore . . . even if he had wanted to.

"You said your brother would not do anything to endanger his chance to marry Jenna," she said quietly. "As well, you said Henry had worked hard to make this a most unforgettable wedding."

"I did say that."

"Listen to what you said. Henry is determined to marry Jenna, and he wants the wedding to be memorable."

"I still am unsure what you mean." He was tempted to add that he might be more able to follow her reasoning if he could set aside his thoughts of pulling her into his arms and tasting her lips again.

Rosie looked out the window, putting one hand on

the frame. "If you check the stables, I suspect you will find that Sir Alexander's swift phaeton is missing."

"Why do you think that?"

He watched her face in the reflection in the windowpane as she said, "I have learned much about the Jordan family in the past few days. I do not believe that either you or your brother do something without an ulterior reason."

"Rosie—"

"No, let me finish." She took a slow breath and released it in a sigh. "When Henry saw Sir Alexander's phaeton, he became excited by its possible speed."

"Yes."

"So he challenged Sir Alexander to participate in a race against your uncle's carriage, which had been the fastest vehicle at Fortenbury Park before Sir Alexander arrived. Sir Alexander's phaeton won by more than a quarter mile, as you may recall."

"I do."

"Do you recall that your brother was grinning even more broadly than Sir Alexander?"

"I recall that."

She whirled and grasped his arms. "Rupert, can't you see what your brother was planning? He wanted to know which was the fastest vehicle at Fortenbury Park."

Rosie watched as understanding filled Rupert's eyes. He pulled away from her and rushed across the room. He must be going to where Mrs. Wallace was lamenting the ruination of her plans for her daughter's wedding.

"Rupert, it is too late," Rosie called to his back. Hurrying to his side before he could open the door, she said in a quieter voice, "Even if Henry and Jenna did not leave until dawn, although my outburst last night gave them the excuse to slip away unnoticed—"

"Yes." He shook his head. "I did not give either my brother or Jenna credit for being underhanded. When I told Henry about how you sang and wrote your own music, he and Jenna devised the perfect diversion."

"Now they have too great a head start. You shall never catch them before they reach Scotland and Gretna Green."

"Gretna Green!" He swore, astounding her for she had never heard him use such coarse language. He did not apologize, showing how upset he was. "How could they be so want-witted? The banns have been read twice here, and the guests await the final reading, and the chapel is ready."

"But think how much more memorable it will be in the years to come that the guests came to Fortenbury Park, and then the bride and groom jilted them by eloping. And there is no chance that anyone will halt Henry from marrying his beloved Jenna."

Rupert stared at her. Then he began to laugh. Loud and hard. He pulled a chair out of the way and sat against the edge of the table.

"How could I have failed to see this obvious solution to Henry's laments?" he asked between laughs.

"You were thinking too rationally."

"And you were thinking with your heart." He held out his hand.

She placed hers on it.

"Rosie, I have been a fool." His fingers closed over hers, and she was certain the joy bubbling within her would overflow at his gentle touch.

"Yes, you have been a fool."

He chuckled again. "I should have learned by now

to judge with my heart what someone in love will do. Using my head in those circumstances is useless."

"Yes."

Drawing her closer, he whispered, "Rosie, there is so much we need to say."

"But first you have to deal with your brother's guests."

"That is simple."

"Simple?" Her laugh was terse, but her fingers rose to brush his freshly shaven cheek. "I cannot imagine any part of this being simple."

"Yet, it is." He cupped her chin. "Just consider. It seems a waste to have these guests here and leave them with nothing to celebrate."

"True. It is nearly Michaelmas. You could have a goose fair at Fortenbury Park and celebrate in the old style."

His nose wrinkled. "I have never fancied roast goose much. I was thinking rather of something that has never been celebrated."

"What?"

"First tell me, what were the last lines of your song?" He began to sing, "*My heart is cold without you, when you are far from me and home,*

*I wonder . . .*"

She continued when he faltered, "*why you have left me unkissed and without your arms around me and why I am now alone.*"

He joined in, his voice weaving a deeper melody to accent hers. "*But I cannot be completely alone while I remember how my name danced each time you spoke it,*

*In the moment before your lips found mine as I gave my heart to you knowing that if you broke it*

*All would be forgiven, for I remember on the day you gave me yours to hold within me,*

*On the same precious day when we spoke our vows melding our hearts, you and I became we.*"

She smiled shyly as the song came to an end. "You do sing very well."

"We sing well together, as we do many other things well together." He dropped to one knee in front of her and took her hand again. Through the frantic beat of her pulse in her ears, she heard him ask, "Will you marry me, Rosie? Before you give me an answer, I do ask you to recall that Michaelmas is the proper time to transplant primroses. Will you leave Dunstanbury and become a part of Fortenbury Park? Say yes, for my love for you has blossomed in the depths of my heart, even when I was trying to deny it. Will you marry me today, Primrose Dunsworthy?"

"Today?" she managed to whisper. "We have no license to wed."

"It would not be a true wedding." He chuckled. "Just a practice one. We would have to wait for the banns to be read or for a special license to be obtained for our marriage to be legally valid. But why not speak the vows before our family and friends today?"

"That makes no sense."

"Sometimes following common sense is the least sensible thing to do." He kissed her right hand, then her left. Running his finger along the fourth finger on her left hand, he said, "But marrying you is sensible. Where better to spend our honeymoon than along the Nile? The time it will take to read the banns will allow me to make arrangements for our travel. What do you say, Rosie? Will you say yes?"

She started to answer but paused as the door flew open. Aunt Millicent came in, then stopped, staring at Rupert on his knee in front of Rosie.

"I . . ." Aunt Millicent gulped, then smiled. "I wanted to let you know that Bianca and Lucian have just arrived. I will go and tell them that there will be no wedding today."

Rosie smiled down at Rupert as she said, "Yes, there will be." Bending, she framed his face with her hands. "A practice wedding with a real one to follow as soon as possible."

He stood and gathered her into his arms. "A practice wedding for Primrose and me."

"Rupert, are you going to continue to call me that?"

"Mayhap, but not right now." He captured her lips, kissing her with a passion that she knew was theirs forever.

# Author's Note

I enjoy hearing from my readers. You can contact me at:

Jo Ann Ferguson
PO Box 26
Whitinsville, MA 01588

Check out my web site at www.joannferguson.com.

Happy reading!